"You're so sweet and sexy and honest with your loving."

McCord's voice was a whisper of midnight velvet. "You always give yourself to me completely, Pru, nothing held back...."

She trembled with both desire and regret as his hands continued to caress her. She hadn't been entirely honest with him. He still didn't know about the baby she was carrying. "I doubt if you were overwhelmed by my generosity when I left you," she murmured instead.

"You did what you had to do. But we'll talk about that ... later." He trailed a string of hot, damp kisses over the curve of her breast and then started working his way down to her navel.

"Oh." Pru clung to his shoulders as she felt the deliciously familiar sensations start to flood her body. All thoughts and fears were swept from her mind as she succumbed to his magical touch....

Jayne Ann Krentz is one of North America's most outstanding romance authors. Though she's written more than forty books—that's an astounding 7 million books in print!—each and every one is special to her.

Fans will be especially delighted with *The Family Way*, Jayne's latest Temptation. In her usual innovative and creative manner, she sets out to prove that history does indeed repeat itself!

Books by Jayne Ann Krentz

HARLEQUIN TEMPTATION

11–UNEASY ALLIANCE
21–CALL IT DESTINY
34–GHOST OF A CHANCE
45–MAN WITH A PAST
74–WITCHCRAFT
91–TRUE COLORS
109–THE TIES THAT BIND
125–BETWEEN THE LINES

HARLEQUIN INTRIGUE

10–LEGACY
17–THE WAITING GAME

The Family Way

JAYNE ANN KRENTZ

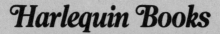

Harlequin Books

TORONTO • NEW YORK • LONDON
AMSTERDAM • PARIS • SYDNEY • HAMBURG
STOCKHOLM • ATHENS • TOKYO • MILAN

Published March 1987

ISBN 0-373-25246-3

Printed in Canada

1

HE KNEW SOMETHING WAS WRONG the instant he turned the silver Ferrari into the curving drive. Case McCord felt his stomach tighten in a cold knot. Pru's snappy little candy-red Ford stood in front of the steps that led up to the wide open doors of the house. There was another familiar car in the drive, an impossibly long, aging, white Cadillac El Dorado, its chrome gleaming in the late afternoon sun. McCord ignored it.

It was the red Ford that alarmed him. The trunk of the car was open, and Steve Graham, the young handyman-gardener McCord had hired a few months ago, was busily trying to fit one of Pru's huge suitcases into the minuscule space.

She meant to go through with her threat, McCord thought in astonishment. She was going to walk out, just as she had said. He couldn't believe it. She wouldn't dare.

McCord slammed the Ferrari to a halt behind the little Ford and wrenched open his car door. Steve Graham paused in his task of trying to wedge the suitcase into the trunk and glanced over his shoulder. The worried expression on his young surf-and-sun-tanned face turned into one of welcoming relief.

"Boy, am I glad to see you, Mr. McCord. Caught an early flight, huh? I was afraid you wouldn't get here in time. It's all a big mess. Pru says she's leaving. For good, she says. Martha's having a fit, and Mr. Arlington is going through your whiskey like there was no tomorrow. The caterers arrived an hour ago, and they're all wandering around looking confused. Pru refuses to talk to 'em and get them organized. Your guests will be here in another couple of hours or so, and Pru says she wants to be long gone by then."

"I have a feeling," McCord said through ominously set teeth, "that Pru isn't worried about leaving before the guests arrive. More likely she intended to get out of here before I got home. She knows there's going to be hell to pay."

Some of the boyish relief disappeared from Steve's expression. He blinked a little nervously at his employer and coughed to clear his throat. "She said you weren't due back until later this evening."

"She made a mistake," McCord informed the younger man. "A big one." He swung around, heading for the steps. His booted feet made a crunching sound as he strode across the graveled drive. He took the steps two at a time and halted for an instant on the top one, turning back momentarily to snap at Steve, "Take that suitcase out of the trunk. Pru's not going anywhere."

"But she said she wanted to be out of here in the next fifteen minutes."

"Take the damned suitcase out of the car, Graham, or you're fired."

Steve Graham had been working for Case McCord long enough to respect the dangerously soft tone of voice, even if he hadn't believed the threat. McCord's voice never rose when he got angry. Instead it went the other direction—low, controlled and ice cold.

In his hurry to remove the luggage from the tiny
trunk, Steve scraped the side of the suitcase. He stared
down at the scratch in dismay. Then he sighed philo-
sophically. Better to have to replace one of Pru's suitcases than risk McCord's fury.

And there was no doubt that Case McCord was furious.

Prudence Kenyon was in the kitchen trying to soothe
Martha Hewett, the housekeeper, when she heard
McCord's footsteps in the hall. Pru closed her eyes in a
brief moment of profound irritation and regret. She
should have moved more quickly today. She shouldn't
have allowed herself to get distracted first by J.P.'s arrival and then by Martha's anxiety attack. Most of all,
she should have guessed that something would go
wrong at the last minute.

Something certainly had gone wrong. McCord had
obviously caught an earlier flight than the one on which
he had been scheduled to return to San Diego.

"Oh, thank goodness, there's Mr. McCord now."
Martha Hewett's tight breathing miraculously began to
ease as she relaxed. She put away the small bottle of
tablets without taking one of the little blue pills inside.
Her eyes brightened with relief and hope. "He'll take
care of everything, Pru, you'll see." She patted Pru's
arm, instantly reversing the roles of caretaker and pa-
tient.

Pru had time for a quick glare at the beaming Martha. The anxiety attack seemed to have completely
disappeared in the wink of an eye, leaving the short,
stout fifty-year-old woman with a serene smile and a
relieved expression in her bright hazel eyes.

"Congratulations on the quick recovery, Martha," Pru observed brusquely just as the kitchen's swinging door was opened with enough force to make the china rattle in a nearby cupboard. The two servers who had arrived with the caterer jumped. Pru didn't bother to turn around. She knew who had just entered the huge, gleaming kitchen. "Perhaps you don't really need that prescription, after all," she said to the housekeeper.

But Martha wasn't paying any attention to Pru. She was staring past her at the big man who was standing in the kitchen doorway, filling the whole room with the force of his presence. "You got home early, Mr. Mc-Cord. I'm so glad. We've got something of a crisis on our hands here. Nothing that can't be handled by the time your guests arrive," she added hastily. "If you could just talk to Pru, I'm sure everything will work out fine. She's a little upset."

"Is that right, Pru? Are you a *little upset*?"

Pru heard the ruthless softness in his voice and raised her eyes briefly toward the ceiling in silent supplication before forcing herself to swing around with a cool smile. "Not in the least, McCord. Everything's under control as far as I'm concerned. I thought Martha was having one of her attacks, but it seems I was mistaken. If you both will excuse me, I'll be on my way."

Boldly she started forward, mentally crossing her fingers in the hope that he would automatically step out of her way. She should have known better. McCord didn't move. He blocked the door as effectively as an armored tank, saying nothing at all until she was forced to halt a few paces from her goal. His dark, hooded gaze swept her from head to toe, taking in the narrow green pullover, snug-fitting jeans and sandals she was wearing. It was very obvious she was not dressed for entertaining the VIPs who were due later that evening.

"So," McCord murmured much too gently as he folded his arms across his broad chest and leaned negligently against the doorjamb, "you meant it. You were really planning to leave."

Pru drew a breath and prayed that only she knew how shaky it was. "Of course, I meant it. We have that much in common, McCord. Neither of us makes false threats. I just left things a bit late, that's all. You weren't due back for another hour."

"You left things much too late." McCord straightened away from the door, his gaze raking Martha and the two nervous men in the catering uniforms. "I have no intention of finishing this conversation in front of an audience. Let's go." He turned to stride back down the hall, clearly expecting her to follow dutifully.

Pru shook her head over the massive arrogance of the man. "I'm afraid I haven't got time for an extended discussion, McCord," she called down the hall after him. "I've got to be on my way. And you'd better see about getting everything organized for your party tonight. There's a lot to be done before your guests arrive."

McCord was already at the open door to the study. He turned to look at her. "To hell with the party. If you've got the nerve to try walking out on me, you can damn well find the nerve to have an extended discussion on the subject. Get in here, Pru, unless you want to have this conversation in the middle of the hall."

"You're not going to find any privacy in the study," Pru warned as she reluctantly started toward him. "J.P.'s in there."

McCord glanced inside the comfortable book-lined room. "Hello, J.P. Didn't anyone ever tell you it's dangerous to get involved in a domestic quarrel?" He walked into the room.

Pru groaned. This was going to be every bit as bad as she had imagined. It would have been so much simpler if she'd got away before McCord had arrived. Now she was stuck having to go through a major scene, one the entire household, assorted caterers and J. P. Arlington himself would witness. Nothing was ever easy when you were dealing with Case McCord.

But, then, she had known that from the beginning.

Pru walked down the hall toward the study as though she were marching toward a court-martial. She told herself she had to remember that it was McCord who had been tried and convicted and that she was judge and jury, not him. McCord had a way of turning the tables in a situation such as this. If she wasn't careful, she would find herself caving in, surrendering, giving up and generally turning into mush.

No one who hadn't been forced to confront McCord could possibly understand just how intimidating and arrogantly forceful he could be, Pru thought. There were a number of factors that contributed to this ability, not the least of which was his sheer size.

McCord was tall, a couple of inches over six feet. He was also hard and lean and strongly, smoothly muscled. His hair was almost as dark as his eyes and closely trimmed in an effort to control a faint wave. It was his eyes that held the key to Case McCord, Pru had often thought. They dominated the blunt, harsh lines of his face.

Those dark eyes held both a razor-sharp intelligence and a simmering passion that was never far below the surface. Intelligence and passion could be a volatile combination in a man, a *lethal* combination. Fury, arrogance and sheer masculine stubbornness were all forces that could be honed to fine degrees by such a mixture. So, too, could sensuality, loyalty and protectiveness.

At times such as this when he was angry, those brilliant, passionate eyes were fathomless pools of cryptic danger. Only a fool would ignore the warning.

But, then, she had been ignoring the warnings that emanated from Case McCord since she had first met him, Pru reminded herself bracingly. That had been six months ago when she had come to work for the Arlington Foundation for Agricultural Research and Development. It was too late to start exercising caution this afternoon.

An observer who knew nothing about Case McCord might have guessed immediately that the man spent a lot of his time outdoors working the land. This afternoon McCord was dressed in a silk tie, gray slacks and a white shirt, but that was only because he'd just returned from an Arlington Foundation meeting in Washington, D.C. The boots he wore were a better clue to his usual clothing style. When McCord wasn't dressed to deal with the scientists, research experts and officials of foreign governments, he generally wore jeans and a casual open-throated shirt. When he was in one of the foundation's experimental fields, he frequently wore a classic Stetson hat.

No, it wouldn't have been hard for an outside observer to guess that Case McCord was at home in rich fertile fields and sun-drenched acres of growing crops. What such an observer might not have understood was that McCord had more than just an intuitive feel for crops and soil and weather. He also had a scientist's extensive training in those subjects.

Case McCord was one of the many research experts employed by the Arlington Foundation. He had joined the foundation staff three years ago, rising rapidly to his present high-level position because, in addition to his scientific training, McCord had a natural talent for leadership. The Arlington Foundation was committed to the improvement of agricultural techniques in developing countries. As its founder, J. P. Arlington was fond of saying in his Texas drawl, people couldn't learn to enjoy the wonders of democracy until they had first discovered the wonders of a full stomach.

At the request of foreign governments and private enterprise, the foundation sent its experts all over the globe. McCord had originally been hired for his knowledge of soil, but his responsibilities now extended into the realm of management and organization. Old J.P. was sharp enough to recognize and make use of the talents he discovered in his staff. Old J.P. was fairly sharp in a number of ways, Pru had discovered during the six months she had been working in the publishing department of the foundation. In his own way, the old man was as smart and dangerous as McCord. The thought of having to enter the study and face both of them was daunting.

She should have said to heck with the evening's social preparations and left McCord's home yesterday, Pru decided. She had been a fool to let her sense of professional responsibility get in the way of her sense of responsibility to herself. Well, the sooner this little scene was over, the better.

Taking a firm grip on her emotions, Pru entered the study. McCord was standing, feet braced slightly apart, in front of his desk, eyeing J. P. Arlington with a cold gaze.

J.P. was, as usual, quite a sight. He was dressed to complement the big, flashy El Dorado parked in the drive. The silver-trimmed, peach-colored western-style suit he wore was not the least bit effeminate on his big frame. He had removed his matching Stetson, displaying his wealth of silver hair. His eyes were gray, and there were a thousand tiny lines radiating out from the corners. Those lines had been induced by years spent under a hot Texas sun. J.P. had inherited land, but forty years ago he'd found the oil under it all by himself.

Arlington was sprawled in McCord's chair, his lizard skin boots propped on the polished desktop. He had a bottle of whiskey open on the low table beside the chair and a glass in his hand. He grinned broadly at Pru as she walked into the room.

"Well, now, maybe we can finally get this little mess sorted out 'fore it goes any farther. I told you to wait till McCord got home, didn't I, girl? Everything's gonna be just fine and dandy now. Nothing like a little communication to work out the problems, I always say. Dealing with McCord can be like dealing with a mule. First you got to whamp him up 'longside the head with a two-by-four just to get his attention. But once that part's done, you'll find he can be right reasonable." J.P. shot a suddenly narrowed glance at the man standing on the other side of the desk. "Talk to her, McCord. I want this little matter worked out as soon as possible.

We've got those ten honchos due here in—" he glanced at the big chunk of gold on his wrist "—less than two hours."

"I'll talk to her," McCord vowed, "but not with you sitting there interrupting every three minutes. Get out, J.P. This is between Pru and myself. It doesn't involve you."

"The hell it doesn't, boy. I need her. She's a damn good journal editor and an even better hostess. If I find myself having to hire someone else to do her job, I'm gonna hold you personally responsible. Now *do* something."

"Get out of my study, J.P." McCord repeated.

Arlington glowered at him and then looked at Pru. "You think you can handle him all by yourself, Pru?"

"Oh, yes," Pru said with a confidence she was far from feeling. "I can handle him."

J.P. hauled himself up out of the chair. "All right. I'll give you two a while to work this out on your own." He glared at McCord. "But I expect results. Don't let Pru here get away, hear me? Blow this, McCord, and I'll have your hide nailed to the hood of my El Dorado." Glass in hand, Arlington stomped out of the room, slamming the door behind him.

Pru watched him go and then resolutely turned back to face McCord. She summoned up a bright, determined smile. "This conversation is a waste of time. I want to be on my way and you're going to have your hands full getting ready for your guests this evening. Martha has full instructions, and all the caterers need is some general guidance, but there's still a certain amount of organizing to be done. I suggest you have Steve set up the bar and tend it. He's getting quite good at that sort of thing. Make sure he puts on a clean white shirt first. Also, when the guests arrive don't let J.P. start telling his stories about his days in the oil fields. You know how he is when he gets on that subject. Be sure to tell Martha to serve the French brandy. This crowd will expect it. Other than that, I'm sure you'll be fine."

McCord leaned back against his desk, his big hands planted solidly on either side of his powerful thighs. His dark eyes were narrowed and grim. "Stop it, Pru. We both know you're not going anywhere."

Pru shook her head sadly. "You're wrong," she said gently. "I really am going to leave, McCord. I told you before you left for Washington that I would be gone by the time you returned."

"You were upset when I left. You didn't mean what you were saying."

"I meant every word," Pru told him. "You just didn't pay any attention."

"I never pay much attention to ultimatums. That's what you were trying to do before I left, wasn't it, Pru? You tried to make me think you were delivering an ultimatum. You should know me well enough by now to know I'd call your bluff."

"It's no bluff. My suitcases are packed. I'm ready to go."

McCord's mouth tightened. "I should let you walk right out that door. It might teach you a lesson."

"I've already learned my lesson, McCord."

"Is that right?" His gaze was mocking. "Which lesson was that? I seem to recall teaching you a number of interesting things during the past few months."

As the warm, embarrassed color blazed in her face, his eyes moved slowly and possessively over her, taking in the sweep of bronzed brown hair that curved just above her shoulders and the clear golden-green of her eyes. He examined the delicate shape of her soft mouth and then went on to the gentle curves of her small breasts. Then his gaze went lower, gliding over the full curve of her hips. There was no doubt about what he was thinking. There was also no denying the memories he was deliberately evoking.

Pru was realistic enough to know that she was not a beautiful woman. She was reasonably attractive in an open, honest sort of way, but she was far from being a riveting beauty. In McCord's arms, though, she had learned what it meant to feel beautiful.

She felt the heat intensify in her cheeks. The past few months with Case McCord had been a passionate interlude unlike anything Pru had ever known in her life. McCord had been smart enough to guess almost at once just how limited her previous sexual experience had been, and he had capitalized on that fact. He had taken great pleasure in teaching her to respond to him. His teaching had been so good that Pru had actually convinced herself that he was in love with her—as in love with her as she was with him. She'd finally had to admit to herself that she'd been wrong.

She held on to her dignity and her self-control as the heated memories flickered in her mind, well aware of the alert, assessing expression in McCord's eyes. She mustn't show any weakness. Not now. McCord would see it and use it.

Determinedly she held McCord's gaze. "The real lesson I learned from you is one my Aunt Wilhelmina spent years trying to teach my sister and me back when we were growing up in Spot, Texas. It's a lesson mothers have tried to teach their daughters since the world began."

"Is that right?" he mocked. "What is this great gem of feminine wisdom?"

"'Give a man free whiskey and he'll get used to the notion of not having to pay for it. It's tough to collect after he's drunk his fill,'" Pru quoted grimly. Aunt Wilhelmina's words echoed in her ears.

McCord's head came up angrily. For an instant his simmering temper threatened to rage out of control. "That's a stupid, juvenile thing to say."

"I tried being very adult and sophisticated about moving in with you, McCord, but it didn't work. Three months ago when you invited, or rather informed me that I was to come and live with you, I told myself that you could be domesticated, that somehow you'd see the wonders of having a good home life and a woman who cared for you. But the more I gave, the more you took. Last week I finally admitted to myself that the situation is hopeless. You're never going to change. You don't want marriage and commitment. You just want all the convenience and advantages of having a woman in your home and in your bed without having to give up anything in return."

"You seemed to be getting something you wanted out of the arrangement," he tossed back. "Why the complaints now?"

"I told you before you left on your trip," she reminded him in a clear, gentle voice. "I came to live with you because I believed our arrangement, as you call it, was going somewhere important. I thought we were building a future together. But after three months under your roof, I realize I was deluding myself." She had deluded herself into thinking he loved her. "As Aunt Wilhelmina would say, 'Weaving daydreams around a man like you is about as useless as putting shoes on a goose.'"

"You're right about one thing. If there was any deluding being done, you were doing it to yourself. You knew I wasn't interested in marriage," he reminded her harshly. "I've never pretended otherwise."

"No," she agreed with forced lightness, "you certainly haven't. Unfortunately, I've decided I do want marriage. And you've made it quite clear I won't ever get that kind of commitment from you."

"So you decided to try to force my hand, didn't you? But it won't work, Pru. I told you that before I left for Washington. There's not a chance in hell I'd let any woman, you included, manipulate me to that extent."

Pru nodded, gazing down at her entwined hands for a moment as she absorbed the pain of his words. "I understand. You've been very honest with me. I was only misleading myself."

"Don't give me that self-deprecating martyr act." McCord came away from the desk and stalked past her to the wide bay window that overlooked the lush garden. "It's not going to work any better than the ultimatum did."

Pru's mouth tightened. "Then I'd better stop wasting your time and mine. I've got a long drive ahead of me. Goodbye, McCord. The past few months have been interesting." She whirled around and headed for the door.

McCord tore away from the window as he realized she really was going to walk out. He caught her arm just as she reached for the doorknob. Yanking her back to face him, he stared down into her composed features.

"You're not going anywhere and you know it. Don't try to play games with me, Pru. You don't stand a chance."

"How many times do I have to explain? I'm not playing a game. I'm leaving. Just as I said I would. Your mistake, McCord, is in thinking I'm trying to manipulate you. I'm not. I'm cutting my losses and getting out. There's no future with you."

"Because I won't put a ring on your finger?"

"Because you're either too much of a coward or you're simply too selfish to make a genuine commitment. I haven't been able to decide which reason applies, but in the end it doesn't matter. Either way I want out."

"You think I'm going to get down on my knees and beg you to stay? You think that by threatening to leave you can get a promise of marriage out of me? Is that it?"

She shook her head wearily and glanced pointedly down to where his fingers were clenched around her arm. "You don't understand, McCord. What's more, I don't think you ever will. You're brilliant when it comes to figuring out how to grow wheat in a desert, but you're just plain dumb when it comes to understanding what it takes to have a real relationship. Please let me go. I told you, I have a long drive ahead of me."

He didn't remove his fingers from her arm. His eyes blazed down at her. "Where is this long drive going to take you? Into some other man's arms? Is that it, Pru? Have you got another man on your string? Someone you've been keeping in reserve in case you couldn't manipulate me into marrying you? Who is he? Does he know about the past few months? Does he know what you've been learning in my arms? How you tremble when I touch you in the middle of the night? Do you think you'll find with just any man what you've found with me?"

"I've got news for you, McCord. You may be good in bed, but that's not enough. Not for me. Now kindly let go of my arm. You're hurting me." For the first time that day she was getting angry. It was risky to let any strong emotion intrude on the composure she had imposed on herself. McCord would seize the opening and use it to his own advantage.

"You're not walking out of here," McCord told her, each word spoken with dangerous emphasis. He glanced down at his hand on her arm and with obvious effort released her. "You can't do it."

"Why not?" She flung open the door. Her self-control was slipping rapidly now. She had to get out of the house.

"You know why not." McCord was striding after her as Pru hurried down the hall toward the front door. *"You can't leave me because you're in love with me, and you know it."*

Pru caught her breath but she didn't pause. He knew. She had hoped to be able to salvage that much in the way of pride, but apparently she wasn't to be so lucky. It shouldn't have surprised her to discover that Case McCord was well aware of the extent of her emotional involvement with him. The man was too damn smart for any woman's good.

There was nothing she could say in response to his challenge. It was the truth, and it was unbearably obvious that they both knew it. Pru saw no reason to add to her humiliation by acknowledging the fact. She went out the front door, aware of McCord hard on her heels.

Steve Graham was standing next to her car, her suitcases beside him on the graveled drive. He looked up anxiously as Pru came through the doorway. His eyes went from her face to the grimly furious expression of the man behind her.

"Haven't you got those suitcases in the trunk yet, Steve?" Pru started down the steps.

"Mr. McCord said not to load them. He said you weren't leaving."

"He was wrong. I'm leaving. If you won't put them in the car, I will."

Steve bent to hoist one of the suitcases. "I'll do it, if that's what you really want, Pru." He cast a defiant glance at McCord, who ignored him.

"If you think I'll come after you on my hands and knees, you're crazy, woman." McCord stood braced on the top step as if he were ready for battle. "This game isn't going to work. Face it and stop behaving like a melodramatic teenager threatening to run away from home because she can't get her own way."

Pru said nothing as Steve slammed the trunk on her suitcases. There was nothing left to say. Without a word she climbed into the Ford, fastened the seat belt and turned the key in the ignition. A moment later she was speeding down the drive.

A glance in her rearview mirror showed J.P., Martha and Steve all hovering around the solid rock of

masculine fury that was Case McCord. After that one
look, she didn't glance back again.

McCord watched the little red Ford until it disappeared from sight. No one around him said a word.
When he finally turned to stalk back into the house he
found himself confronting three accusing faces.

For an instant no one spoke and then Martha said in
a forlorn voice, "She's gone."

"That's obvious, isn't it?" McCord snapped. "I suggest you get busy, Martha. Apparently there are a lot
of things to be done before our guests arrive. You
haven't got time for one of your anxiety attacks. Steve,
I understand you're going to handle the bar this evening. Go set it up. Try not to leave bottles and glasses
lying around tonight the way you leave the gardening
tools scattered around the grounds. Why are you three
looking at me like that? This isn't my fault, you know.
It was Pru who threw the temper tantrum and walked
out two hours before a party."

"Don't put the blame on her," J.P. muttered. "She
didn't want anything more than what any nice young
lady from Texas has got a right to expect from her man.
You've been as happy as a bull in clover for the past few
months. Got everything you wanted, didn't you? But
you never noticed that sweet little Pru was hurtin' inside. It was only a matter of time before she upped and
left. Surprised it took this long. Don't know what I'm
gonna do for a hostess, let alone a good journal editor
now."

"I'm going to miss her," Steve remarked wistfully.
"We were just getting the garden into shape. She won't
be here to see how the tomatoes turn out."

Martha sniffed and reached for a handkerchief. "She was certainly a very understanding person." She blew into the scrap of linen. "Not everyone understands what it's like to have anxiety attacks."

McCord's eyes glittered with frustrated fury. "Kindly ash-can the maudlin postmortems. I don't want to hear them. We've got a lot to do in the next two hours. Get moving, all of you." He forged through the small group on the steps and strode down the hall into the study. Not even J.P. tried to stop him.

Once inside he slammed the door closed, walked over to his desk and picked up the bottle of whiskey J.P. had left behind. There was a spare glass sitting on the small shelf beside the desk. McCord splashed the amber liquid into it and then moved to the window.

She was gone. Afternoon sunlight still streamed through the windows, but the place already seemed empty and dark. It was as though she'd walked out of the house and turned off all the lights behind her.

McCord's hand tightened into a fist around the glass of whiskey.

2

A WEEK AFTER HER GRAND EXIT from Case McCord's home, Pru found herself stretched out on a lounger beside her sister's pool in Pasadena. A large table umbrella sheltered her from the direct glare of the sun. The entire Los Angeles basin was simmering in the warmth of the early summer heat, and Pru found herself thinking of how pleasant the gardens in McCord's home would be on a day like this. His lovely house on a hillside in La Jolla just north of San Diego had a cooling view of the ocean. She was going to miss it on days such as this.

The view from McCord's gardens wasn't the only thing she was going to miss, she reflected as she watched her small niece and nephew splashing happily in the cool crystal water of the pool. Even as the thought went through her mind she was inundated with another small wave of pool water. Pru was already so damp from the children's exuberant actions that she was considering bestirring herself for another dip.

Before she could make up her mind on the matter, Annie Gates stuck her attractive blond head around the kitchen door and called out to her sister. "Hey, Pru. Want a glass of lemonade?"

"I do," seven-year-old Katy yelled from the pool.

Not to be outdone, her brother, Dave, echoed the appeal. "So do I."

Annie wrinkled her nose in affectionate admonishment. "Are these the same two kids who didn't have room for brussels sprouts at lunch?"

"I'm hungry now," Katy assured her mother.

"Me, too," Dave repeated predictably. He was almost two years younger than his sister, but he was quick to pick up on her lead. By watching Katy, he was rapidly learning that assertiveness pays in this world.

Pru grinned at her older sister. "If you're making lemonade, you'd better make it in quantity."

"Heck, if the response is this good, I might just start charging for it." Annie disappeared back into her gleaming modern kitchen. When she came outside a few minutes later, she was carrying a large plastic pitcher of lemonade and four plastic glasses. "Okay, everyone, come and get it."

Katy and Dave needed no second invitation. They bounced out of the pool to collect their glasses and then went over to their child-sized lounge chairs to drink the lemonade.

"Just what I needed," Pru told her sister as she reached for a glass.

"You're not the only one." Annie sat back in a webbed chair and propped her sandaled feet on the end of Pru's lounger. "Somebody turned the heat on early this year. Almost reminds me of summer in Spot, Texas. Almost, but not quite. How are you feeling?"

Pru smiled and sipped her lemonade. "Fine. Any reason why I shouldn't?"

"No, of course not." Annie sighed. "Sorry if I'm being overprotective. It's just that since you don't have a husband to fuss over you, I feel obliged to fill the gap."

"I appreciate it," Pru said gently, "but it's not necessary. I really am okay."

Annie eyed her shrewdly. "Or at least as okay as any woman can be when she finds herself unmarried and pregnant?"

"I'm twenty-seven years old, Annie. I'm not some naive teenager who's got herself into trouble."

"No, you're a rather naive twenty-seven-year-old who's got herself into trouble. That bastard."

Pru shook her head. There wasn't much she could say. Annie had formed her own opinion of Case McCord. She was a protective older sister, and she was not inclined to take an understanding or charitable view of the man who had got Pru pregnant. "I've told you, Annie. He doesn't know I'm pregnant."

"Would it have made any difference?" Annie challenged.

Pru hesitated. "I don't know. I didn't put it to the test. If he wasn't interested in marrying me for myself, I certainly didn't want him marrying me because of the baby."

"You're too proud for your own good, Pru."

"I can handle this on my own. Lots of women do."

"That doesn't make it right!"

"I know." Pru shrugged. "But these things happen."

"You should never have got involved with him." It wasn't the first time Annie had made the observation. "The day you phoned to tell me you were moving in with him I knew you were headed for trouble. He used you."

"At the time," Pru said reflectively, "I thought he needed me. I know he wanted me. I hoped he loved me."

"Well, of course he *wanted* you. You fell right into his palm, didn't you? Men are always willing to take what's available, especially if they don't have to pay for it."

Pru's eyes widened and then her smile turned into outright laughter. "You sound just like Aunt Wilhelmina."

"Be grateful Aunt Wilhelmina doesn't know about this situation yet. When she finds out she's going to have hysterics."

"No, she won't. She'll simply come to the conclusion that there's bad blood in the family. She won't be surprised. She undoubtedly suspected it all along," Pru said humorously, thinking of the iron-spined, rigidly upright aunt who had raised her and her sister.

"She always meant well. And she tried hard to make up for mother's, uh, shortcomings." Having lived away from Aunt Wilhelmina for several years now, Annie was willing to be broadminded on the subject. "Someday she'll reap whatever heavenly reward exists for martyred spinsters who wind up having to raise their sister's illegitimate children," Annie added dryly. "When are you going to tell her you not only lived with a man for a few months, but you also went and got yourself pregnant by him?"

"Not until I have to," Pru said bluntly. "Aunt Wilhelmina hasn't mellowed much with age, and you know it. I'd just as soon not listen to all her lectures on men drinking their fill of free whiskey and milk without feeling obliged to pay for the booze or buy the cow."

"I'll tell you something," Annie said quietly, her eyes going to her daughter. "Every time I think of Katy growing up and starting to date, I find myself inclining toward Aunt Wilhelmina's point of view. I know it sounds old-fashioned and cynical, but I want to tell her not to risk giving herself to a man until she's very, very sure of him."

"Until he's proven himself by putting a ring on her finger, you mean."

"Face it, Pru. You wouldn't be in the situation you're in today, if you'd followed Aunt Wilhelmina's advice."

Pru regarded her sister evenly. "Are you going to tell me you didn't sleep with Tony until you were married? Because I won't believe you. You were head over heels in love with him and he couldn't keep his hands off you."

Annie had the grace to blush and then she smiled. "Well, at least I was reasonably sure of our feelings for each other before we made love. That's more than you can say, isn't it, Pru? You knew from the beginning that you were taking a huge risk when you got involved with Case McCord."

"At least he was honest with me," Pru said quietly. "He told me from the start that he had no intention of getting married."

"You didn't believe him?"

"I thought," Pru murmured, "that I could change his mind. I thought that deep down he had the makings of a good family man. He's very much a homebody, you know. The only evenings he didn't spend at home with me were the ones he spent traveling for the foundation. I would swear that during our time together McCord was totally faithful to me."

"You weren't together all that long. Maybe the novelty hadn't had a chance to wear off."

"You're turning very cynical these days, Annie."

"I get more than cynical every time I think about what he's done to you. I get furious."

"I knew what I was doing and I knew the risk I was taking," Pru pointed out. "I also knew when I told him I wanted to make serious plans about our future that he would probably explode."

"When did you confront him?"

"The day I got home from the clinic after finding out for certain I was pregnant. I handled it all wrong. I know that now. But I was feeling a little emotional at the time."

"I'll bet you were," Annie said with great feeling. "So you gave him an ultimatum?"

"McCord doesn't respond well to ultimatums. He was due to leave the next day on a trip to Washington, D.C. I told him that if he wouldn't agree to settle our future, I wouldn't be around when he got back. I guess I managed to convince myself that he really did love me and he would realize it when faced with the prospect of losing me."

"You figured wrong."

Pru shrugged. "He assumed I was trying to manipulate him, to force his hand. And in a sense I suppose I was."

"As long as you were trying to force his hand, you should have pulled out all the stops," Annie said candidly. "You should have told him you were pregnant."

Pru closed her eyes, remembering the stormy scene in the study before she'd left McCord's house for the last time. "I couldn't do it. I wanted him to want me. I didn't want him offering marriage out of a sense of obligation. I think he might have done it. He's got a rather eccentric but quite rigid code of honor. But everyone knows that a marriage that takes place solely because of an unplanned pregnancy doesn't have much chance of lasting. The truth is, he meant what he said in the beginning. He doesn't want to get married. He doesn't want a long-term commitment. I should have taken him at his word."

"How much longer could you have stayed with him on his terms if you hadn't got pregnant?"

Pru's mouth tightened. "I don't know, Annie. I wanted more from him than he was willing to give. I wanted it long before I discovered I was pregnant. I longed for a commitment right from the start. I guess Aunt Wilhelmina's teachings went deeper than I thought."

"It's not the fault of Aunt Wilhelmina," Annie declared roundly. "It's just the way you are. You're the kind of woman who would give herself completely in a relationship. You're generous, warmhearted and utterly loyal. Some part of you wants the same kind of response in exchange. You tried to force that response from a man who has no intention of ever giving it. That was your first mistake. Getting pregnant was your second. How did it happen, anyway?"

"The usual way."

"This isn't a joke, Pru. What went wrong? Did your contraceptive fail?"

Pru took another long sip of lemonade. "Not exactly. There was one night when we didn't use anything. I was unlucky."

"But why did you take the chance?"

Pru's brows climbed as she regarded her sister over the rim of the glass. "You want a blow-by-blow account?"

Annie smiled wryly. "Of course not. I just wondered how you could have forgotten when it's obvious neither you nor McCord wanted any unexpected events."

"McCord had been out of the country for ten days."

"Ah." Annie nodded sagely. "Ten days of abstinence made him careless, hmm?"

"No," Pru said thoughtfully. "Ten days of surveying the problems of the drought in Africa got to him. You can only imagine what it's like over there, Annie. McCord had to witness it firsthand. The Arlington Foundation is setting up programs in a couple of African countries to teach basic agricultural skills to the farmers. It's also designing some more sophisticated training programs for researchers and scientists over there. But McCord didn't stay in the cities. He went out into the country to see the land for himself. The land . . . and the people who are dying on it."

Pru broke off, remembering the weary, bleak expression on McCord's face the night he had returned. The grim reality of what he had seen had taken its toll. McCord might not be capable of making a commitment to a woman, but he was very committed to his work.

"I think I'm beginning to get the picture. He was worn out and probably feeling rather helpless in the face of such an overwhelming problem. Add to that a good case of jet lag and you have a man who is not thinking as clearly as he should about certain things," Annie concluded with the first trace of understanding she had yet shown for McCord.

"He went straight to bed. So did I." Pru took a deep breath. "But he woke up in the middle of the night and he, well, things just happened." She didn't try to explain the rest. There was no way to describe the urgent, primitive hunger that had blazed in McCord's eyes in the shadows of the big bed that night. No way to explain her own awareness of his need.

After ten days of looking at death, McCord had been reaching out for life. He had reached for Pru, and she had gone into his arms without a moment's hesitation.

"I see," Annie said softly. She was silent for a long moment, her eyes on her two healthy, well-fed children who were highly unlikely to ever know the meaning of drought and famine. Then she reached for the lemonade pitcher. "And so your whole life is suddenly changed."

"Yes."

"Well, as Aunt Wilhelmina always says, 'It's not the big things in life that generally do you in, it's the little stuff. You're more likely to get bitten by a tick than by a rattlesnake.'"

"I'm not sure McCord would like being compared to a tick, but I can understand what Aunt Wilhelmina was trying to say," Pru murmured.

There was silence under the umbrella for a long while as both women watched the children scramble back into the pool. Pru relaxed again and leaned back in the lounger. Her hand went unconsciously to her still-flat stomach. She indulged herself by trying to decide if her baby would have McCord's dark hair and fathomless eyes.

"You can stay here as long as you like, Pru," Annie finally said sincerely. "Tony won't mind."

"You've both been very generous, but I won't be imposing on you much longer. I think I'll take the apartment we looked at yesterday."

"The one near CalTech?" Annie nodded. "It's a good area. If you get that job on campus that you applied for on Monday, everything will be perfect. Or just about perfect," she amended practically.

"Speaking of Tony," Pru ventured.

"Umm?"

"You haven't told him yet about my, er, condition, have you?"

"No, of course not. I promised I wouldn't, didn't I?"

"Yes. Sorry."

Annie smiled wryly. "You won't be able to keep it a secret for long, Pru."

"I know. It's just that it's all so new. The whole idea of being pregnant is very strange. I need time to adjust."

"I understand." Annie was about to add something else when she was interrupted by the distant sound of the doorbell. "Sounds like we've got visitors. I'll be right back. Keep an eye on the kids for me."

"Sure." Pru watched her sister slip back into the house and then turned her attention to Katy and Dave who were busy playing king of the mountain with an inflated plastic raft.

"Aren't you coming back into the pool, Aunt Pru?" Katy demanded from her precarious perch on top of the bright blue raft. Dave was busily trying to bounce his sister off into the water.

"In a few minutes," Pru called back. She folded her bare legs and sat forward so that she would have a better view of the children's active play. Both kids were at home in the pool, but they were still small and vulnerable in so many ways. Annie and Tony were very protective of them.

She would protect her own baby, Pru reflected, feeling wise and maternal, but she wouldn't overprotect him or her. Children needed room to test themselves. Room to grow and make their own mistakes.

Up to a point.

Pru decided that if she had a daughter she would do her level best to keep the young woman from making the kind of mistake Pru herself had made, just as Aunt Wilhelmina had tried to keep Pru and Annie from making the kind of mistake their mother had made. Women were probably fated to pass the warning along from one generation to the next forever. And there would always be a few who would ignore it to their cost.

Pru was pulled out of her philosophical reflections by the sound of her sister's voice. Annie was agitated about something. Pru couldn't hear the words, but she caught the tone. Automatically she glanced toward the kitchen door in time to see it swing abruptly open.

It wasn't Annie who came through the door first. It was Case McCord.

Pru's glass of lemonade tilted precariously in her hand, spilling a couple of sweet, sticky drops onto her bare thigh. She was hardly aware of the small splash of coolness on her sun-warmed skin. Her whole attention was riveted on the man coming toward her.

A dangerous, deceptive flare of hope suddenly came alive somewhere deep inside Pru in that moment, and she realized that it had never really died. A part of her had been nourishing that reckless hope since the day she had walked out of McCord's La Jolla home.

His eyes went to her face instantly, and Pru was jolted by the impact of his dark, assessing gaze. She sat very still on the lounger, not quite daring to move. The reality of McCord's presence was almost more than she could accept. The strength and will and driving determination of the man were palpable forces surrounding him.

With a searching hunger that she hoped didn't show in her eyes, Pru examined him. He was dressed in his usual casual style: jeans and a long-sleeved shirt, the cuffs of which had been rolled up on his forearms to reveal the strong, sinewy muscles. His near-black hair was slightly tousled, as if he'd recently run his fingers through it in an impatient gesture. His boots sounded loud on the tiled patio that edged the pool. He headed toward Pru with long, ground-eating strides.

Pru was dimly aware of Annie hastening along in McCord's wake, snapping at him in an infuriated voice rather like a small, enraged terrier. "Damn it, you have no business barging in here like this. My sister has a right to decide whether or not she wants to see you. I won't have you harassing her, do you hear me?"

"Mommy? What's wrong?" Katy stopped her rough-and-tumble pool play to glance curiously at the newcomer. Beside her, Dave, too, went still. His blue eyes took in the stranger with a great deal of interest.

"Nothing's wrong," Annie declared forcefully. "This man says he wants to see your aunt, that's all. Go back to your game." Annie called ahead to Pru. "I didn't know who he was, Pru, until he was inside the house. I'm sorry about this. You don't have to speak to him if you don't want to, you know."

McCord spoke for the first time as he came to a halt in front of Pru. "She'll talk to me," he announced in his soft, even voice. "Won't you, Pru?"

Slowly Pru unfolded her legs and sat up on the edge of the lounger. Her eyes never left his face. "What are you doing here, McCord?"

His smile was wry, rueful and strangely gentle. His dark eyes were shadowed and deep. "You know the answer to that, don't you, Pru? I came to find you."

Her pulse was beating a little too fast, a little too strong. "Why?"

He crouched in front of her so that his gaze was on a level with hers. "I think you know the answer to that, too. I've come to take you home with me. It's where you want to be and it's where I want you to be."

She shook her head, feeling dazed. She couldn't believe he was here. Case McCord was not the kind of man to run after a woman, any woman. "I don't know what to say," she whispered.

He reached out and caught hold of her, his strong fingers closing warmly around her small hand. "You're not usually at a loss for words. You certainly weren't the day you left." He stood up and tugged her to her feet in front of him. "Why do you look so shocked, honey? Didn't you expect to see me one of these days?"

"No," she blurted honestly as her mind began to clear itself of the strange, disoriented sensation. "I assumed you meant what you said when you made it plain you had no intention of coming after me. You always mean what you say, McCord."

"I can make mistakes like anyone else."

She heard the faint, familiar arrogance behind the words. "Oh, I don't doubt that for a minute. I just wouldn't expect you to admit those mistakes. At least not so quickly."

He chuckled softly and tugged at her hand. "Let's go someplace where we can talk. It's almost five-thirty. Go change your clothes and I'll take you out for drinks and dinner. We don't need an audience." He indicated the two children and Annie, all of whom were watching the encounter with great attention.

His words jarred Annie out of her unwilling silence. She looked at her sister. "You don't have to go anywhere with him, Pru."

"I know." Pru looked at McCord. "Give me a reason, McCord."

"To come with me?" The hint of arrogance was stronger now. It was evident in the tilt of his brows and the hardening edge of his smile. He wasn't accustomed to having to justify his actions. "Do I need to give you a reason? Don't you want to come with me, Pru?"

"Not if you're under the impression that everything between us can be put back the way it was. I wasn't having hysterics the day I left. And I didn't walk out in a rage. I left because it was the best thing for me to do under the circumstances. I haven't changed my mind."

"I have," he told her simply.

She stared at him. "You've changed your mind?"

"You've made it clear you won't settle for anything except marriage. I want you back. If the only way I can have you is to marry you, then there's nothing left to argue about. Go change your clothes, Pru. We'll go somewhere private and discuss marriage."

Her mouth trembled when she tried to find a response. No words came into her head. Pru turned to look at her sister, seeking some hint of how to handle the bizarre situation. But Annie was looking distinctly thoughtful.

"Go get dressed, Pru," she said quietly. "McCord is right. You can't hold a private discussion with this kind of audience hanging around."

Pru glanced at McCord. There was a steady, watchful expression on his face, as if he were afraid she would panic and run.

The knowledge that he half expected her to react in such a ridiculous manner sent a shot of adrenaline-inspired strength through Pru's system. With a cool little nod, she excused herself and walked across the patio toward the sliding glass doors that opened onto the living room. A moment later she vanished inside.

McCord watched her go, aware that his body was already tightening just at the sight of her sweetly rounded bottom outlined by the red bikini she was wearing. God, he had missed her. This past week had been one of the most frustrating and miserable he had ever spent.

"She was quite sure you wouldn't come after her," Annie remarked, interrupting McCord's reverie.

He snapped his attention back from the sliding glass doors and turned to look at Pru's sister. She didn't look much like Pru, he decided. Annie was a sassy-haired blonde with blue eyes while Pru's hair was much longer and darkened into a warm shade of bronzed brown. He liked the golden-green of Pru's eyes better, too, McCord thought. He saw the protective hostility in Annie's gaze and sighed inwardly. He wasn't surprised.

"I didn't properly introduce myself earlier, Ms Gates."

"Don't worry about it. I've figured out who you are. Are you serious about marrying Pru, or is this just a trick to get her to go back to San Diego with you?"

McCord felt a brief rush of fury at the clear sisterly skepticism so visible in Annie's face. Coolly he repressed it. "I'm serious about it. I wouldn't have mentioned it otherwise."

"When?"

He looked at her blankly. "When what?"

"When are you going to marry her?" Annie asked impatiently.

"As soon as possible." He challenged her silently and was briefly startled when Annie merely nodded.

"Good," she said. "I think it's for the best." She turned back to the pool. "All right, kids. Time to get out and get ready for dinner."

Katy and her brother moved reluctantly to the steps and clambered out. "Is he going to have dinner with us?" the little girl asked, her eyes on McCord.

"No," her mother said briskly. "He's going to take Aunt Pru out to dinner. Run along now." She turned back to McCord. "Have a seat, Mr. McCord. My sister will be out in a minute." She started toward the house but halted abruptly when McCord spoke behind her.

"I'll take care of your sister, Annie," he said quietly.

Annie's gaze flickered over him in quick assessment. "It's not going to be as easy as you think, McCord."

"What won't be easy?"

"Convincing her to marry you. You've already done too good a job convincing her you don't want to marry her." She turned away again and continued on into the house.

McCord stood by the rippling pool and thought about the problem. Annie was right. He'd done a hell of a job convincing Pru he would never marry her. He'd been honest about his feelings on the subject of marriage right from the start, even though at the time he'd worried about losing her because of it. But she'd eventually come into his arms with all the honeyed, passionate generosity of her nature. And then she'd moved in with him and proceeded to turn his house into a home.

As far as McCord had been concerned, the arrangement between himself and Pru had had a more solid foundation than did most marriages. He'd been angry and stunned when she'd suddenly insisted on discussing their future. Having his sweet, generous-hearted, passionate Prudence turn into a willful, demanding woman who dared to threaten him with an ultimatum had infuriated him. He had immediately decided that the most effective way of teaching her that he would not be manipulated by a woman was to call her bluff.

But she'd meant every word of her ultimatum.

For the first full day after Pru had walked out, McCord had told himself she would be back. She loved him—he was sure of it. When the burst of feminine temperament had died away, he was certain she would come flying back to him.

He'd still been reeling from the shock of having her carry out her threat when the bill from the women's clinic had arrived. The moment he'd torn it open and examined the contents, a great deal had suddenly become excruciatingly clear. On her own, Pru might very well have come back to her lover. But she was no longer on her own. She was pregnant.

She was carrying McCord's baby; the baby of a man who had arrogantly claimed he had no interest in marriage. Belatedly McCord had realized exactly what was behind Pru's decision to leave. She'd been forced to assume that if he couldn't abide the thought of marriage, he would be even more unwilling to accept the fact that he was a father. Still, she'd gathered her nerve and taken the risk of pushing for marriage. When he'd rejected her, she'd done the only thing she'd thought she could do under the circumstances. She'd left.

Tonight he would have to woo her all over again, soothe her uncertainties and fears until she felt safe in surrendering to him once more. Because there really was no option now. The instant he had realized she was pregnant, McCord's whole world had realigned itself.

No longer could he allow his past to shape his present.

McCord stood alone on the sun-warmed tiles of the patio and thought of that past. For three years now he had cut himself off from everything and everyone he had known from cradle to young manhood. He had told himself he could live without those things and those people, even pretend they didn't exist. He had walked away from the stubborn, proud man who was his father, from the raw memories of his dead fiancée and the unborn child who had died with her. He'd also walked away from his inheritance.

But now he was going to marry and have a baby. Everything had changed.

3

PRU ORDERED FRUIT JUICE instead of her customary glass of wine when the cocktail waitress came by to take the order. McCord glanced at her with an amused expression.

"Have you decided to live up to your name tonight? Afraid to let your brain get cluttered with alcohol?"

"Under the circumstances, I think a measure of prudence makes sense." She had recovered her equilibrium now. As she sat across from him in the cozy bar that adjoined the dining room of the expensive restaurant McCord had chosen, Pru felt she was finally able to regard him in a rational, cautious manner.

It was much too soon to confess that she was pregnant and that she was avoiding alcohol for that reason only. She had to take this slowly and carefully. McCord, as usual, was moving very fast. The last time he had moved this fast, she had found herself agreeing to live with him.

McCord reached across the small table and covered her hand with his own. His eyes were hooded in the shadows, but the dark fire in them was quite evident to someone who knew him as well as Pru thought she did.

"You don't have to worry, honey. If we wind up in bed tonight, it will be because you want to be there, not because I got you drunk and seduced you. Give me some credit. I've never used that tactic on you."

"You never had to," she heard herself admit ruefully. The fruit juice and McCord's whiskey arrived before he could respond. When the waitress left, Pru studied her drink.

"Does that bother you, Pru?" McCord asked softly. "The fact that you wanted me as much as I wanted you?"

Her head came up, her eyes serious and a little troubled. "I'm not ashamed of the way I felt about you, but I think it made things easy for you and difficult for me."

"You're in love with me, aren't you, Pru?" His gaze was very direct, allowing no room for maneuvering. "That's the bottom line. It's the reason you went to bed with me the first time and it's the reason you finally agreed to come and live with me."

She forced a small shrug. "You always seem to have all the answers, don't you, McCord?"

"Are you going to deny it?"

"No. There's not much point. It doesn't matter, anyway. You'll believe what you want to believe. The real question is how you feel about me."

He blinked at the cool way she had turned the tables on him. A reluctant smile of admiration edged his mouth for a few seconds. "I want you back. I want you in my bed and in my home. I realize you need the security of marriage in order to be happy. I'm willing to give you that security."

She pushed her glass of fruit juice aside and leaned forward to ask the only question that mattered. "Do you love me, McCord?"

He was silent for a moment. "I don't know," he finally said with blunt honesty. "What do you think?"

She shivered. "I think you do, but for some reason you're going to have a hard time admitting it. I wish I knew what that reason is. It's been driving me crazy ever since I first met you."

It took a lot to startle McCord, but he definitely looked surprised by her thoughtful words. "What the hell are you talking about?"

She smiled and sat back in her chair, studying him. The scooped neck of her narrow white cotton knit dress slipped slightly to one side, revealing the delicate hollows and curves of her shoulder. The candlelight gleamed on the thin gold chain she wore around her neck. In the soft light her eyes were almost gold. "Don't you realize how little I or anyone else for that matter knows about you, McCord? Oh, J.P. knows you're brilliant in your area of expertise and that you have a talent for getting things done in the field. Martha knows you like peanut butter pie and that you detest sweet after-dinner liqueurs. Steve knows you like gardens and lots of healthy growing things around your home."

"What about you, Pru? What do you know about me?"

She made a small movement with her hand. "I know you went to good schools, that you're committed to the work of the foundation, that you've been faithful to me since we've met."

He smiled faintly. "What makes you so sure of that?"

"I don't know. I just am."

He nodded. "Go on with your list."

"Well, I've learned a hundred little things about you—"

"Including how to please me in bed."

She tried to ignore the deliberate look in his eyes. "You're a good teacher. That's not the point, McCord. What I was about to say is that, while I know a lot of small, inconsequential things about you, there are a lot of important things I don't yet understand."

"Such as?"

"Why you were so adamantly against marriage, for one thing." There was a heartbeat of silence before Pru asked the next question. "Have you ever been married before, McCord?"

"No. I was engaged three years ago."

She chewed on her lower lip, considering the cryptic response. "And things went wrong?"

"Very wrong."

"You're...you're not still carrying a torch for her, are you?"

"She's dead, Pru. She was killed in a car accident. No, I am definitely not carrying a torch for her." The tone of his voice made it clear that that was all he intended to say on the subject.

Pru absorbed the implications of the abrupt words. "Is that why you didn't want to marry? Too much trauma left over from your first engagement?"

He lifted his whiskey glass and took a slow swallow. "What happened in the past doesn't concern you, Pru."

"Maybe not, but I'm entitled to know why you've suddenly changed your mind about marrying me," she tossed back.

He lowered his glass. "I've told you why I've changed my mind. I want you back and you've made it clear marriage is your price."

Pru shuddered, closing her eyes in pain. She sat very still. "This isn't going to work, is it? I'm sorry, Mc-

Cord. Please believe me, I never intended to set a price on myself and demand that you meet it. I never wanted this kind of situation to develop between us. I wish I could make things easy for both of us. Unfortunately I can't live with you. Not any longer. But now I know I can't marry you, either. Not as long as you view the whole thing as a business transaction. I refuse to sell myself to you in exchange for a ring."

"Pru . . ."

She ignored him, getting to her feet in a swift movement and reaching for her small purse. "You don't have to worry about me, McCord. I'll call a cab."

"Damn it, Pru, sit down." He was on his feet before she could get around her chair. His hand closed over her wrist, exerting just enough pressure to force her gently but firmly back down into her seat. His eyes blazed with masculine irritation. "You've already walked out on me once in front of an audience. I'm not going to let you do it a second time. You've shredded my ego and my pride pretty thoroughly, lady. I don't need another dose of your feminine temperament. Isn't it enough for you that I'm here on my hands and knees trying to offer marriage?"

She stared at him, straining against the hold on her wrist. When she realized it wasn't going to slacken she settled back into her chair. He released her and sprawled into his own seat, glaring at her.

There was a measure of tense silence before Pru's sense of humor finally surfaced. "On your hands and knees, McCord? Please excuse me, I hadn't realized you were actually groveling. I had the distinct impression you were here to order me to marry you."

His mouth twisted wryly. "It would certainly make my life simpler if I could. Do you know what I've been through in the past week? From the moment you left, Martha and Steve have barely spoken to me. J.P. has delivered at least one lecture a day on how to treat a good woman. You'd think I'd had you chained to my bed, forced to live in sin for the past three months from the way everyone acts. Even if I could convince you to come back and live with me without benefit of marriage, I'm damn sure J.P., Martha and Steve wouldn't allow it. They all think I've had my wicked way with you long enough. Now that you've escaped my clutches, they hope you'll stay out of my reach until you've forced me to do the right thing."

"I had no idea," Pru murmured dryly, "just how many people in this world still harbored the same sentiments as my Aunt Wilhelmina when it came to such things as living with a man versus marrying him."

McCord groaned. "This is the famous aunt who gave you the lectures on not sleeping with a man until you'd got him to the altar?"

"That's her." For some reason Pru was suddenly feeling more cheerful. A certain tension between herself and McCord had just been broken, she realized. A large measure of the ease they usually experienced in each other's company had been restored. She began to relax for the first time that evening.

"It occurs to me," McCord observed slowly, "that there are a few things I don't know about you. I hadn't even met your sister until today. Is there anyone else in your family?"

"Just Aunt Wilhelmina. She lives in Spot, Texas."

"Your parents?" he prompted gently.

"My mother is dead," Pru said quietly. "She was killed shortly after I was born. She was in a car with a man who was very drunk at the wheel. He might have been my father. They were on their way to Mexico. I like to think they were going to get married over the border. A childhood fantasy of mine."

"Lord, Pru, I didn't realize—"

"It's all right. I never really knew her. Annie suffered more than I did. She was five years older than me, and she still has a few memories of our mother."

"And her father?"

"A trucker. He was long gone by the time Annie was born. My mother was apparently a very reckless young woman when it came to choosing her male companions. She was also very desperate to get out of Spot, Texas. Apparently she hoped some man would help her. Two illegitimate children were the result. My aunt is very much afraid there's bad blood somewhere in the family."

"What do you and your sister believe?"

Pru smiled gently. "That my mother was born dirt poor and that on two occasions she tried desperately to escape her poverty by getting involved with men she hoped would marry her. She guessed wrong both times."

"So it was your aunt who raised you?"

Pru nodded. "My aunt was always very proud of the fact that she didn't take the low road out of poverty. She got herself an education. Eventually became a grade school teacher. She wound up supporting two young children on that salary." Pru paused and then said slowly, "It's very difficult growing up under the care of someone who makes no secret of the fact that she was forced to make great sacrifices for you. Frankly, there were times when I wished she'd just let the state take Annie and me." Pru smiled. "But of course Aunt Wilhelmina would never have done that. She is an honorable woman who always knows her duty and does it."

"While making sure that everyone around her knows she's doing it?"

"Exactly."

"I know the type." McCord's mouth lifted in amusement.

"Well, I can hardly complain. Aunt Wilhelmina is a good woman. She devoted her life to making certain neither Annie nor I followed in our mother's footsteps. She was very strict with us, but she got us both through school and college. And she understood when the first thing we wanted to do after graduation was shake the dirt of Spot, Texas, from our feet. She had a few doubts about the wisdom of first Annie and then me going to California, but she figured she'd done her best to instill basic values. Now it was up to us to keep our own lives in order. She was thrilled when Annie married Tony Gates. She could stop worrying about one of us, at least. She comes out to see them frequently. I think she's mellowing a bit as she grows older. She seems to enjoy Annie's kids."

"I take it you never told your aunt about your relationship with me?" McCord held up a hand before Pru could respond. "Forget I asked. It's obvious you wouldn't let her know you were living with a man without benefit of a wedding ceremony unless you absolutely had to. I imagine she's the type who would go through the roof?"

"More likely she would just decide bad blood will out," Pru corrected him.

McCord shook his head in chagrined wonder. "I knew it wasn't easy for you to make the decision to move in with me, but I had no idea just how much you had to overcome in your own mind to do it."

Pru thought about that. "It was something of an unstable situation right from the start. But I might have been able to make it work, if only—" She broke off abruptly.

"If only what, honey?" McCord held the verbal door open, trying to coax her inside. Perhaps now she would tell him about the baby. But she shied away from mentioning it. He wondered why, but he said nothing. It was, after all, her surprise. She had a right to spring it on him.

"Never mind. McCord, what are we going to do?"

"Get married."

"I'm not sure. I just don't know. There are so many things to be considered. So many things I've realized I don't know about you."

"Don't worry about it, Pru. You love me, and I don't want any other woman except you. It has recently been brought home to me in no uncertain terms that you need a marriage license in order to be content. I'll see that you get one."

She was right about some elements of the situation. There were a lot of things she should know about him, McCord decided, but tonight wasn't the time to tell her. She was still feeling tense and uncertain in spite of the more relaxed atmosphere between them. He didn't want to try to explain his family situation at the moment. That could come later. Right now he had to concentrate on gentling her back into his life. "Honey, you know me as well as anyone else in the world does. Better, if you want the truth. You know I've never lied to you. You have to believe me when I tell you that I want you with me."

"But marriage?"

He saw the undisguised longing and the hope that lit her eyes. She really did love him, he thought. She was just afraid to admit it aloud. He was touched by the fact that she hadn't tried to use the baby to force his hand. It made him realize how deep her pride ran.

During the past week he'd begun to acknowledge to himself that marriage might not be such a bad idea after all. The notion had been growing on him, he realized. Like a fungus, as J. P. Arlington would have said. McCord discovered he rather liked the idea of having Pru tied to him legally as well as emotionally. Something about the concept suited the possessive side of his nature. He wondered why the realization hadn't occurred to him earlier. Probably, he admitted silently, because there had been no need to think about it. J.P. was right. McCord had been as happy as a bull in clover. There had been no reason to think about altering a situation that had suited him perfectly.

"Yes, Pru. Marriage. It's what you want, and I'm willing to go along."

She didn't seem thrilled with the way he had phrased it, but she didn't bounce out of her chair and run out the door, either. She was silent for a long moment. When she spoke, her voice was very soft and tentative.

"Have you ever . . ." Pru stopped, cleared her throat and tried again. "Have you ever thought about having children?"

McCord smiled with all the reassurance at his command. "I figure if we're going to get married, we might as well go the whole route. And the sooner the better. We're not getting any younger, are we? I think we'd make good parents, don't you?"

"Yes," she said happily, "I think we would."

There was a trace of relief in her eyes, but she said nothing. McCord didn't push.

He concentrated on letting the evening flow gently after that. Deliberately he turned the conversation toward more general topics, filling her in on news of the foundation and giving her Steve Graham's report on the garden.

"One of these days I'm going to find a way to teach him to put away his tools," McCord said with a grimace as he finished describing the progress of the tomatoes.

"He loves gardening and he's learning so much from you. You know you enjoy teaching him," Pru pointed out. "Why make such a fuss about a minor bad habit?"

"It's hard on the tools and someone could get hurt, that's why," McCord growled.

Pru grinned. "It's such a small thing. Don't worry about it."

"See if you're still saying that after you step on a rake," McCord said.

Because it was his nature to settle matters in a clean, straightforward fashion instead of letting them stay muddled, McCord would have preferred to keep up the pressure on Pru. Now that his own decision had been made, he was impatient with Pru's uncertainty. But he was increasingly aware that she was teetering on the brink, and he was equally sure he knew which way she would fall when the time came.

As the meal drew to a close, McCord forced himself to consider his immediate options. He had a simple choice to make. He could either try to coax her back to his hotel room or he could take her to her sister's house and leave her with a chaste, gentlemanly kiss.

There was no question which option he favored. He had spent the evening in an uncomfortably tantalizing state of semiarousal. One touch was all it would have taken to bring him to the explosive point. It was obvious Pru was being very cautious about touching him. He wondered if that meant she was as close to flash point as he was. He thought she might be. After all, he had spent several months getting to know her intimately, learning exactly what it took to make her shiver with excitement and in the process developing a sixth sense for reading her responses.

She was his woman, McCord thought, and he knew her well. If he pushed just a bit tonight he could push her right back into his bed. It was where he wanted her, and he had a hunch that, even though she wasn't quite prepared to admit it yet, it was where she wanted to be.

As they rose to leave the restaurant, his eyes rested for a moment on the delicate curve of her breasts beneath the narrow cotton knit dress. When she walked ahead of him toward the door, he was vividly conscious of the subtly provocative sway of her hips. It was going to be fascinating to watch the changes her slender body went through during pregnancy.

He suddenly discovered that the thought of his babe curled safely now in its warm nest was more intensely exciting than he would have believed possible. McCord ached to make love to the woman who was carrying his child. The fierce, possessive sensation jolted him, making him catch his breath. As if she sensed something was wrong, Pru glanced back with a small frown.

"McCord? Is something the matter?"

"No," he said tightly, knowing now which option he had to choose. "There's nothing wrong. At least, nothing I can do anything about tonight." He caught her arm as they moved out onto the sidewalk. The silver Ferrari was parked half a block down the street. "It's time I got you back to your sister's place. It's getting late."

Pru inhaled the warm, balmy air, aware of the comforting strength in McCord's arm as he guided her down the street. "You're going to take me straight home?"

"I didn't say that. I said I'm going to take you straight back to Annie's. Your sister's place isn't home for you, Pru. Your home is with me."

"You sound very sure of that."

"I am sure," he said as he stopped beside the Ferrari and opened the car door. "And when you're sure, too, I'll take you home. Until then, I'll just take you back to Annie's house."

She looked up at him warily as she slid into the seat. He smiled faintly at the shielded expression in her eyes and then closed the car door very firmly before she could decide what to say in response. As she watched him walk around the front of the Ferrari, Pru felt a sharp pang of longing. She wanted to touch him when he folded himself gracefully into the driver's seat, but she didn't quite dare. Surreptitiously she touched her still-flat stomach instead.

Without a word McCord guided the Ferrari down the palm-lined street that wound through Annie's affluent neighborhood. It wasn't until he parked the car in front of the Southwestern-style house that he finally spoke.

"I'll come by for you in the morning. We can spend the day at the beach." He studied her, one arm draped over the wheel as he waited for her response.

Pru tried to force herself to think clearly and logically but couldn't. "All right," she heard herself say. "That would be nice."

He nodded once and climbed out of the car. When he got her to the front door he stopped. She knew at once he was going to turn around and leave immediately. For the first time that evening Pru reached out to touch him.

"McCord?"

"What is it, Pru?"

"I... Don't you want to come inside? You haven't met Tony."

"I can wait until I know for certain I'm going to be a member of the family." He leaned down to brush his mouth against hers. The kiss was fleeting and rigidly restrained.

Pru made a small sound, a combination of protest and longing that was almost lost in the soft sounds of the night. If McCord heard it, he gave no sign. He lifted his head almost at once, as if the touch of her lips burned him.

"The doorbell," he prompted.

Pru blinked. "What?"

"Ring the doorbell."

"Oh." She fumbled in her purse. "It's all right. I have a key."

He took it from her and inserted it into the lock. When she was over the threshold, he nodded good-night and turned to go back down the walk toward the Ferrari.

Pru was torn between wanting to scream and wanting to laugh. Slowly she closed the door and leaned back against it. Annie appeared in the hallway, her concerned eyes full of questions.

"Somehow," Annie said calmly, "I wasn't expecting you home tonight."

"Ah, that's because you don't know Case McCord very well." Pru came away from the door. "The man is smart. Smart enough to know when to push and when to let his victim fumble her own way right into the trap."

"You don't seem too upset about his tactics."

Pru smiled secretly. "I'm not too upset because I think he really means it, Annie. I think he really does want to marry me."

Annie grinned. "I think you're right. How long are you going to keep him dangling?"

Pru touched her stomach. "Not long. I just want enough time to be sure." She sighed in soft wonder. "I didn't think he'd come after me, Annie. I honestly thought I'd never see him again."

"Then you don't know him as well as you think you do. I took one glance at his face this afternoon when he forced his way through the front door and I knew immediately he wasn't leaving here without you."

SHE KEPT HIM WAITING two more days. They spent one of those days at the beach and another at Disneyland.

It was fun doing frivolous things with McCord again, she thought on the drive back from Disneyland. The realization made her glance at McCord who was negotiating the intricacies of the Los Angeles freeway system.

"How much time do you have, McCord? Won't J.P. be needing you?"

McCord grinned, but he didn't take his eyes off the traffic. "J.P. gave me strict instructions not to come back without you."

Her eyes widened. "I didn't know he was that concerned about losing one little journal editor."

"I think it's your hostessing abilities he misses most. He's accustomed to having you organize the cocktail parties and brunches and dinners the foundation gives. He dreads having to figure out how to do it on his own. You've spoiled him. With the first annual foundation ball coming up in a couple of weeks, he's desperate. You were the one who talked him into it, don't forget. Remember how you assured him he'd get a fortune in contributions to the foundation if he put on a first-class charity ball? You've been taking care of everything up to this point, and the thought of putting the affair on without you around to supervise is enough to traumatize him. The only thing J.P. knows how to do is barbecue a steak. He's overwhelmed by the idea of caviar and canapés."

"He could find another hostess."

"He wants you back." McCord paused a fraction of a heartbeat and added, "So do I." Then he smiled. "J.P. says that without you, I'm about as useful to him as, uh . . ."

Pru kept her gaze on his hard profile and asked sweetly, "About as useful as mammary glands on a bull?"

"Something like that. J.P. was a bit more graphic."

"I'll bet. That's the sort of thing J.P. or my aunt would say." She sat quietly for a few more minutes, staring out the window. Then she nodded to herself. "All right."

McCord risked a quick glance, his eyes rapidly searching her face. "All right? You're accepting my proposal?"

"Yes." She smiled. "If you're sure you want to marry me, McCord, then, yes, I accept."

He snapped his attention back to the freeway traffic. "You picked a fine time to tell me."

"Any complaints?"

"No, ma'am," he assured her fervently. "I'll take what I can get."

"You are sure, aren't you, McCord?" she asked quietly. "I couldn't stand it if you . . . if you changed your mind or came to regret marrying me. I truly don't want to force you into this."

"I know that, Pru. Stop worrying. I'm very sure I want to marry you."

That evening Pru and McCord told their news to Annie and Tony. Annie laughed and hugged her sister. Tony, a slender, good-looking man in his early thirties, shook McCord's hand and offered him a drink.

"You'll need one before you talk to Aunt Wilhelmina," he informed McCord.

"I didn't know I was scheduled to meet her." McCord accepted the whiskey and settled onto the sofa next to Pru. He eyed his new fiancée quizzically. "Don't tell me she's in the neighborhood. I thought she lived in Texas."

It was Annie who responded. "She does. But we'll have to call her later and tell her Pru's getting married. She'd never forgive Pru otherwise."

Pru made a face. "No loss."

"Now, Pru, you know you don't mean that." Annie grinned. "What's the matter? Afraid McCord might change his mind after he's dealt with Aunt Wilhelmina?"

"It's a distinct possibility."

Tony chuckled. "You'll survive, McCord."

"How bad is she?" McCord asked dubiously, but there was laughter in his eyes when he glanced at Pru.

"Just imagine every battle-ax of a teacher you ever had in grade school all rolled into one. All those teachers who kept you after class to finish your work and all those who sent you to the principal whenever you put one little finger out of line. And don't forget all the ones who made you feel like an absolute idiot whenever you blew a math test or a spelling exam. Then there were those whose idea of sex education was to warn you that you could get a girl pregnant by dancing too close to her. You get the picture?" Tony took a swallow of his drink. "But I made it through the inquisition, so I expect you to pull yourself together like a man and do the same."

"Inquisition?" McCord asked blandly.

"Sure." Tony enlightened him. "She'll ask you how much money you make, if you own your own home, what your future prospects are, and whether or not you have health insurance and a pension plan. Then she'll want to know if you're marrying Pru because you've got her in trouble."

Pru went utterly still, aware of the fierce warmth leaping into her cheeks. She shot a quick, painful glance at her sister. Annie shook her head very slightly, silently reassuring Pru that she hadn't told Tony about the baby. Pru drew a long breath of relief. Then she looked at McCord. He seemed oblivious of her tension. He was laughing ruefully at what Tony had just said.

"Has anybody ever tried telling Aunt Wilhelmina that the answers to all those questions are none of her business?" McCord asked.

"Are you kidding? Tell Aunt Wilhelmina to mind her own business? What a mind-boggling thought." Tony managed an expression of stunned amazement.

Annie held up a hand to stop her husband. "Enough. You'll scare him off before he even talks to her. Don't worry, McCord. Tony is exaggerating. He has a weird sense of humor."

"I'm glad to hear it," McCord said. "Why don't we make the call and get this over with?"

Pru spoke up, glancing at her watch. "It's almost nine o'clock back in Texas. Why don't we wait until tomorrow?"

"Nervous, honey?" McCord was laughing at her. "Afraid I'll chicken out after I've talked to Aunt Wilhelmina?"

"Well, no, it's just that I—"

"Don't worry," he said softly, some of the amusement fading from his eyes. It was replaced by a suggestion of grimness. "Whatever problems you've got with Aunt Wilhelmina are nothing compared to the problems I've got with my family. At least you're still speaking to your aunt."

"What are you talking about?" Pru stared at him in astonishment. "What family? You've never mentioned anyone, McCord."

He picked up the small designer telephone that was sitting on a nearby end table and handed it to Pru. "Call your aunt."

"But what about your family?" she demanded.

"I'll take you to meet them after the wedding. I'm not fool enough to let you meet them ahead of time."

"But McCord—"

"One gauntlet at a time, Pru. Call your aunt."

Pru's fingers felt cold and numb as she dialed her aunt's number in Texas. Something was very wrong. It occurred to her that there were still too many things she didn't know about Case McCord.

4

THREE NIGHTS LATER Pru stood in front of the expanse of mirror that lined one wall of the elegant inn bathroom and wondered why she was feeling so nervous. It was McCord who waited for her out in the bedroom. The same McCord with whom she had lived for three months. The McCord who had taught her the wonders of her own sensuality. The McCord who could make her feel incredibly beautiful in bed.

The McCord who had got her pregnant.

It wasn't as if he were a stranger. He had been her lover and now he was her husband. Soon he'd be the father of her child. Her attack of bridal jitters didn't make sense.

They had been married that afternoon in a small, simple ceremony with only Annie and Tony present. Considering the questions and uncertainty and the painful emotions Pru had been through during the two weeks leading up to the wedding, the ceremony itself was something of an anticlimax. She had been aware of McCord's strong, steady voice as he made his vows, heard her own soft words and then, quite quickly, it was all over.

McCord had settled her into the Ferrari afterward and turned to say farewell to his new brother-in-law. Annie had leaned down to speak to her sister through the window.

"You still haven't told him about the baby, have you?" Annie had whispered.

Pru had shaken her head, smiling. "No. This is a special time. The wedding and the honeymoon are for us, McCord and me. I want us to be able to concentrate on each other for a day or two. Then I'll tell him."

"I understand," Annie had said, grinning. "I think I like your husband, Pru. He certainly handled Aunt Wilhelmina well the other night. I thought I'd collapse laughing when she started grilling him on the phone and he just listened and smiled and said he'd have his banker write her a letter of reference. Poor Wilhelmina. I can just imagine her expression. There she was asking all those pointed questions and McCord just brushed past them."

"He can be very good at ignoring what he doesn't consider important."

"The best part was when she asked him if he'd got you in trouble," Annie had said with a rueful grimace. "Tony was right. Aunt Wilhelmina really did ask that. I couldn't believe it."

Pru had flushed slightly, remembering McCord's response. Although she and the others hadn't been able to hear the question, they had all known when it had come because McCord, phone to his ear, had rested his amused gaze on Pru's scarlet cheeks.

"Don't worry about it, Aunt Wilhelmina," he'd advised. "If there's trouble, it's nothing I can't handle."

For just an instant Pru had wondered if McCord knew about the pregnancy. The intensity of his gaze had almost burned her. But then she had told herself that he couldn't possibly know.

Aunt Wilhelmina had been almost too outraged to respond for several seconds. In the end, however, when the phone had been handed back to Pru, she'd pronounced herself reasonably satisfied with McCord.

"Sounds like he's got both feet on the ground, Pru," Aunt Wilhelmina had declared. "Bold as brass and proud as the devil, but that's not altogether bad in a man. He also sounds slicker than a greased hog on ice. Be grateful he's marrying you. He's the type who could have talked you right into bed without bothering with the ring. Call me when you get back from your honeymoon."

"Well?" McCord had asked, not appearing overly concerned. "What's the verdict?"

Pru had cleared her throat. "She says you sound slicker than a greased hog on ice and that I should be grateful you're marrying me because otherwise you might easily have ruined me."

McCord had winced. "Ouch. The woman does have a narrow view of the world, doesn't she?" Then he'd grinned wickedly. "Are you grateful that I'm marrying you, Pru?"

She'd batted her eyes in mock admiration. "Oh, yes, terribly grateful. Words can't begin to express my gratitude."

McCord had laughed and wrapped one large hand around the nape of her neck. He'd pulled her toward him and dropped a kiss on her nose. "As if I had a choice."

She hadn't known how to take that comment, but decided he'd meant it as a joke.

After the ceremony, McCord had driven her up the coast past Ventura. They'd checked into a beautiful, rambling inn near the ocean and Pru had been delighted with the fireplace, the huge bath and the luxurious furnishings of the small suite. The perfect honeymoon hotel, she'd decided exuberantly.

But now she was unaccountably nervous, and she didn't know why. One thing was for sure—the longer she delayed going out into the bedroom, the more anxious she got.

She took one last look at the flowing lines of the pale yellow, low-necked negligee she had bought for her honeymoon and then straightened her shoulders and opened the connecting door.

McCord was standing in front of the window, gazing out over the darkened sea. He was stripped to the waist, and he had taken off his shoes. The jeans he'd put on after dinner rode low on his hips, and his broad, smoothly muscled shoulders gleamed a faint gold in the dim light of the bedside lamp.

He'd opened the bottle of champagne he'd ordered earlier from room service, and two fluted glasses stood on the table beside him. When he heard the sound of the bathroom door being opened, he turned to confront his bride. His eyes were endlessly dark and unfathomably deep, but the shimmer of possessiveness in them was unmistakable. Pru halted in the doorway, a little disconcerted by the directness of his gaze.

McCord smiled faintly and reached for the bottle of champagne. He filled the two glasses, picked them up and came deliberately across the room to offer one to Pru. She took it with fingers that trembled ever so slightly and managed to return his smile.

"I know," McCord said with soft reassurance as he stood looking down at her. "I'm a little nervous, too."

"I suppose that's one of the advantages to having lived with a man before you marry him," Pru murmured. "He knows you well enough by the wedding night to guess how you're feeling when you come out of the bathroom."

"There is a certain comfort in familiarity, isn't there?" McCord tipped the champagne to her lips and urged her to take a sip.

Pru thought of all the current advice that encouraged pregnant mothers not to drink and contented herself with barely wetting her tongue. Then she wrinkled her nose as she realized she really didn't care for the taste. Odd. Normally she enjoyed good champagne.

"If we're so familiar to each other, why are we feeling nervous?" Pru asked, looking up at McCord.

He shrugged. "Probably because, when all is said and done, it's different being married."

Pru felt a wave of unease go through her. Her eyes widened in the soft light, the underlying anxiety plain in them. "McCord, are you very, very sure this is what you wanted?"

He took the unfinished glass from her fingers, set it down beside his own and then wrapped his strong hands around her shoulders. She was fascinated by the masculine certainty that blazed out at her from his eyes.

"Oh, yes, my sweet Prudence, this is what I wanted. It just took me a while to realize it." He brushed his mouth lightly over hers, and then his grip on her shoulders tightened.

Pru's smile was tremulous with relief as he pulled her up against his hard chest. Overwhelmed by the depth of her feelings for him and the tremendous relief she felt at finally being with McCord again, Pru clung to him. Her head rested against his bare shoulder, and she closed her eyes as the warm, musky scent of him washed through her senses.

"I never thought I'd see you again," she whispered.

"You should have known better." He dropped the softest of kisses into her hair.

"You said you wouldn't come after me."

"I was madder than hell at the time. Besides, I thought you were bluffing. I couldn't believe you'd really leave me."

Pru felt suddenly guilty. Her arms tightened around his waist. "I'm sorry. I thought I had to leave."

"I know," he said gently. "After getting to know you all these months, and after talking to your Aunt Wilhelmina, I can only conclude it's a miracle you stayed with me as long as you did before you demanded a more settled arrangement. You're the kind of woman who wants to make a commitment. And you want the same thing in return. I should have realized that months ago. I should have guessed what would happen as soon as I knew you were in love with me."

She turned her face toward his shoulder and astonished both of them by nipping his skin with her small white teeth. "Beast. What makes you so sure I'm in love with you?"

"I don't know. Since the first time I took you to bed, I've felt very sure of you." His hold on her tightened as she started to protest. "I know that sounds arrogant, but it's your own fault, you know. You never tried to hide your responses from me. That's why I didn't pay any attention when you threatened to leave. I thought you loved me too much to carry out the threat."

"I didn't think I had any choice."

His hands moved slowly and luxuriously along her slender back as he gentled the tension in her. "I know, sweetheart. For what it's worth, I think you were right. We couldn't have gone on much longer the way we were. It was time to settle the future." His dark voice was a whisper of midnight velvet against her skin as he cradled her chin in one palm and lifted her face for his kiss.

The last of Pru's uncertainty left her in a soft soundless sigh as she felt the reassuring touch of his mouth. The hunger and the need in him rippled through her, touching all of her senses. McCord wanted her with the same limitless desire she had always sensed in him.

His desire wasn't really unlimited, she thought with womanly anticipation. It only seemed like that in the beginning because the sensual demand emanating from him was so huge. When McCord took her in his arms, Pru felt as though she had been swept into a deep, torrential waterfall of masculine need. But she knew from past experience that she could turn the thundering cascade into a slow, lazy river of contentment.

His mouth moved heavily on hers until she made a tiny sound of pleasure and opened her lips. McCord was inside at once, tasting her, provoking her, exciting her as only he could. Pru shivered in his grasp.

"It's been so long," McCord muttered against her mouth.

"Only a couple of weeks."

"Seems like forever." He deepened the kiss again until she was leaning into his strength. When he felt her fingers clenching and unclenching on his shoulders, he groaned and scooped her up in his arms.

"McCord?" She looked up at him with wide, trusting eyes that were luminous with her love.

"I told myself I was going to make tonight very special. If you look at me like that before I've even got you to the bed, I won't be able to last long enough to do this right." He put her down on the turned-back sheets of the wide bed and stood gazing at her for a long moment.

Pru smiled. "Don't you know it's always special with you? You always seem to be able to last long enough to do things right."

He grinned abruptly, a slanting, teasing, excitingly wicked grin of pure masculine anticipation. His hands went to the snaps of his jeans. "I guess that's another wedding night advantage we've got, isn't it, honey? We don't have to worry about whether we'll be able to please each other." The jeans landed on the floor, and McCord stepped closer to the bed.

Pru's pulse quickened at the sight of his lean, hard body. She had seen him aroused before, of course, but the sight of his strong, heavy manhood never failed to send a shudder of excitement through her. "I should be used to seeing you naked." Her fingertips glided softly over his hard thigh as he came slowly down beside her. "But somehow I don't think I'll ever get completely accustomed to sharing a bedroom with you."

McCord chuckled, a deep, sexy, richly amused sound. "I know. I like the way you always blink and stare for a couple of seconds whenever you see me nude. Does unmentionable things to my ego." He leaned over to kiss the hollow of her throat. "Don't worry. You should get over that particular hang-up sometime during the next sixty years or so."

Pru sank her fingertips into the thickness of his hair and looked up at him with a sudden, earnest intensity. "You think we'll be together that long?"

His eyes blazed. "We both made a promise and a commitment today, Pru. Now that the deed is done, there's no turning back for either of us. I don't make promises or commitments lightly, and neither do you. We're going to make this marriage work."

The words were a vow and Pru accepted them as such. With a soft, throaty sound she put her arms around his neck and pulled his head back down to hers. She felt his fingers at the laces of her nightgown even as his mouth urged her lips apart once more.

The shimmering fabric of the gown was pushed aside until McCord had freed Pru's small, full breasts. When his palm grazed lightly over one nipple, drawing it into a hard peak, Pru gasped. He drank the small sound of desire from her lips and then he slid his warm hand to the other rosy crest. By the time he was finished with the light, teasing touch, Pru's breasts were exquisitely sensitive.

She moaned into his mouth and sought the hard contours of his body with impatient hands. Her fingertips laced through the mat of curling hair on his chest, sliding across the flat, male nipples until McCord was the one who was making the soft sounds of need. His hand slipped down to her stomach, and he spread his fingers possessively over her.

"You're so sweet and sexy and honest with your loving," he murmured. "You always give yourself to me completely, nothing held back."

She trembled, deeply aware of the warmth of his palm. It occurred to her that she hadn't been completely honest with him recently. He still didn't know about the baby. "I doubt if you were exactly over-whelmed with my generosity two weeks ago when I walked out," she whispered.

"There was nothing ungenerous about your actions. You did what you felt you had to do. You were feeling desperate. I understand that now." He trailed a string of hot, damp kisses over the curves of her breast and then he started working his way down to her navel.

"Oh, McCord," Pru heard herself say as she lifted herself against his hand, "I'm so glad you decided you wanted to marry me, after all. It could never be this good with anyone else. I would have been so lonely...."

"So would I." His fingers went lower, moving to the place that shielded her most exotic secrets. With uner-ring expertise he explored the flowering heart of her desire. His fingers glided through the flowing warmth there.

Pru clung more tightly to the strong, reassuring bulk of his shoulders as she felt the deliciously familiar, yet ever new sensations that were starting to flood her body. McCord's hands had always held magic, she thought. It was such an indescribable relief to know she wouldn't have to live without that magic now.

With a gentle assertiveness that would not be de-nied, McCord probed farther, urging her thighs apart until he could tease and tantalize every hidden fold. When his rough fingertips found the source of the dampening heat between her legs, Pru cried out softly. Then she turned her head into his shoulders and used her teeth against his skin with sweet, feminine sav-agery.

"Ah!" McCord's response was tight with his barely leashed need. "Every time I start thinking you're all sweetness and light, you manage to remind me that there's a healthy dose of she cat in you."

"You should know. You're the one who brought her out into the open." She heard his sexy laughter as she ran her hand down his body to find the waiting shaft of his manhood. When she touched the throbbing, rock-hard evidence of his desire, he groaned and murmured hot, dark words in her ear.

The sensual demand in his voice was as enthralling and as exciting as his touch. Pru stirred restlessly, opening herself more invitingly.

"That's the way I like to see you, sweetheart. Hot and wet and needing me."

She tightened her intimate hold on him, teasing him as he was teasing her. "I do need you, McCord. So very much." She was aching with the longing he had elicited. When she moved against him, tightening her arm around his neck, she caught a fleeting glimpse of gold. It was the ring he had put on her hand that morning. She loved him, she thought. She loved him so much that she could never leave him again.

"It's only been two weeks and I feel like I'm going to explode." McCord sounded wryly annoyed as his control rapidly slipped away from him. "I shouldn't be surprised. You've had this effect on me since the first moment I met you. I think I'm going to like being married. It's going to be good to know that you really do belong to me, legally as well as every other way. I wonder why I didn't realize it before?"

She couldn't answer that question for him. Pru could only be glad that he had asked it. "Love me, McCord," she begged, wrapping her arms around him and drawing him closer. "Please love me."

He said nothing, but his thigh slid aggressively between her legs. McCord found her throat with his lips as he lowered himself along the quivering length of her. She felt his solid male shaft touch the smooth, silky skin of her inner thigh and then his hand was clasping her rounded bottom, lifting her. Now she could feel the waiting, blunt hardness of him, but he didn't push himself into her.

Pru was suddenly aware of the stillness in him and opened her lashes to see a waiting fire in his eyes. She had never known him to hesitate before. His body was shuddering with the force of his need. But he was holding himself in check.

"McCord?"

"You do it, Pru. Guide me. Take me inside, sweetheart. Let me know you want me and show me exactly how you want me. I'll be as slow and careful and gentle as you want me to be. I promise."

She shook her head once in wondering confusion. This was a new side to the McCord she thought she knew so well. His consideration touched her deeply. She sank her fingers into his hair and smiled. "I want you to be the way you always are with me. You've never, ever hurt me, McCord."

He closed his eyes for an instant. When he opened them again, the dark gaze burned her. "Sometimes I'm a little rough with you."

She didn't understand. "Only in a very exciting way. Have I ever complained?" Her smile was unconsciously provocative.

"No." His voice was uneven. "You always respond to me so beautifully. I'm addicted to your responses, don't you know that? But I thought that now you . . . that is, I figured you'd want to take things a little slower, a little more gently than we usually do."

Her smile deepened. "Because this is my wedding night? Don't worry, McCord. All I want tonight is what I've always had with you. But if you'd like a little direction . . ." She slid one hand down his body, found the poised weight of him and gave him the guidance he said he wanted.

McCord realized he'd made a mistake when he nearly exploded in her hand. The touch of her fingers on his pulsing, throbbing manhood was almost more than he could stand at that moment.

"That's enough," he gasped. He reached down to pull her hand out of the way. "Forget it. Bad idea. I'll never last if you don't let go." He caught her hand and cradled it in his own as he kissed the center of her palm. Then he released her wrist and gripped her shoulders. He had waited long enough. She said there was no need to be extra careful or gentle tonight. He'd trust her to know what was best under the circumstances. She wouldn't do anything that might put the pregnancy at risk.

The image of Pru starting to grow round and full with his baby filled his mind even as he drove into her with all the pent-up hunger that had been gnawing at him for the past two weeks. It was an unbearably exciting picture that threatened to shred what was left of his self-control.

As if she sensed the powerful need coursing through him, Pru responded in kind. Her body shivered and trembled in his grasp. Her eyes were tightly closed against the waves of sensation that were steadily tightening her slender softness. McCord craved the feeling of her body when she was vibrating with sensual reaction the way she was tonight. The effect on him was stronger than that of any drug. It filled his senses and sent ripples of pleasure and power through him.

He could never get enough of her, he thought dazedly as he surged into her. He slid one hand back down beneath her to hold her hips and then pushed himself so deeply into her that he felt as though he were a part of her.

"Yes, McCord. Yes, my love. Please, please, oh, yes, *please*."

He heard the breathless, squeezed way the last *please* sounded as it hovered on her lips and then he felt her body lock convulsively around his. She was beyond herself, her senses spinning out of control and, as always happened, she pulled him into the whirlwind with her.

"Oh, God, *Pru*." Whatever else he said after that was lost as a shuddering release whipped through him. McCord held on to Pru with a grip that couldn't have been shaken loose by dynamite. He held her to him with violent strength as together they shared the moment of exquisitely wordless communion and shimmering passion.

They stayed wrapped together in the depths of the wide bed as long moments passed and their bodies slowly spiraled back to reality. McCord waited until he felt his breath return to normal before he reluctantly eased himself away from Pru's warm, soft body. Her hand moved in a vague, languid gesture, and he saw the flare of gold on her finger.

"My wife," he said quietly. The strange sense of possessiveness and satisfaction he had been experiencing since he'd put that ring on her finger this morning welled up in him again. He looked down at her love-gentled face. "You're my wife now."

"You're my husband." Her eyes were filled with a dreamy wonder. She snuggled closer. He could feel the sleepy trust in her as she nestled in his arms.

"I'm glad," McCord said with crystal-clear realization, "that it's all settled this time. You won't run away from me again."

It was a statement, not a question, but Pru didn't seem to notice or care. She dropped a tiny kiss on his damp chest and shook her head resolutely. "Never again."

As she fell asleep in his arms, McCord wondered in affectionate amusement just how much longer she was going to wait before she told him about the baby.

PRU AWOKE THE NEXT MORNING with a distinctly queasy feeling in her stomach. She felt momentarily disoriented, and then the full impact of her vague nausea hit her.

She had thought she was going to be one of the lucky ones who didn't suffer from morning sickness. Apparently she had been wrong.

"Oh, Lord." She lay very still, staring at the ceiling and hoped the feeling would pass.

At the sound of her softly muttered words, McCord stirred sleepily. His heavy arm was resting on her stomach. Pru wished badly that he would remove it.

Normally she loved the intimate way he cradled her while they slept. But this morning the weight on her stomach seemed to be contributing toward her unpleasant queasiness.

"Are you awake already?" McCord turned onto his side and lazily threw one foot over her ankle. His hand on her stomach moved deliberately.

The small movement was enough to turn the queasiness into a definite feeling of sickness. Pru was suddenly sure that just lying very still and hoping was not going to save her.

She hadn't even told McCord. What a way to break the news to him.

"Honey?" McCord studied her through narrowed eyes. "Are you okay?"

"I have to go to the bathroom," Pru explained urgently. She was already shoving back the covers and swinging her feet over the edge of the bed.

"I see." His words were dry, tinged with a faint trace of humor.

But he spoke to empty air. Pru was already through the bathroom door, slamming and locking it shut behind her. She dashed for the porcelain bowl.

The next few minutes constituted a very unpleasant time. It was made even more unpleasant for Pru because she couldn't decide which was worse, the morning sickness or the knowledge that this was a stupid way to tell McCord she was pregnant. She'd planned to do it in a much more dignified, romantic style. Perhaps over a candlelit dinner or while she was undressing for bed.

She flushed the toilet just as McCord started pounding on the door.

"Pru? Are you sick? What's the matter? Open the door, honey."

It occurred to her that she had never been sick around him. She was generally as healthy as a horse. Aunt Wilhelmina hadn't raised any weaklings.

"I'm okay, McCord. I'll be out in a few minutes."

"Open the door now, Pru." Indulgence and concern were rapidly being replaced by firm command in McCord's voice.

Pru knew that voice. She also knew she wasn't up to defying him this morning. The nausea had passed, but she still felt weak. It wasn't a good idea to argue with McCord unless you were feeling in top form. It was difficult enough to do it even then. Wearily Pru unlocked the door.

It swung open immediately. McCord stood on the threshold, hands on hips, glaring at her with fierce concern. "What's going on?"

"I just woke up feeling a little nauseous, that's all."

He examined her pale, wan face. "I can see that. Feeling any better now?"

"I'll live. I think."

He appeared to be about to say something more and then changed his mind. His voice softened. "Go lie down for a while, honey. I'll take my shower and we can talk about it when I get out. You should be feeling better by then."

Talk about what? she wondered. How did he know she wanted to talk about something important? She couldn't quite make sense of the words, but she didn't feel like contradicting him. A few minutes more in bed might be enough to get her through this lingering unpleasantness. She could spend the time figuring out how to tell him he was about to become a father.

He guided her gently to the bed and tucked her back in. Then he smiled enigmatically down at her. "I'll be out in fifteen minutes." He leaned down and kissed her forehead and then he sauntered into the bathroom.

Pru stared after him, perplexed. He was being altogether too casual about finding his new wife sick in the bathroom first thing in the morning. She wondered how long it would be before he began to put two and two together. McCord wasn't a stupid man. In fact, he was generally alarmingly smart.

She assimilated that bit of data and light began to dawn. Pru began to wonder which of them had been dismayingly slow recently.

He knew.

The realization went through her mind like wildfire. Pru shoved back the covers again and sat bolt upright. "It's impossible," she breathed. He couldn't know. No one knew except her sister, and she trusted Annie not to have betrayed her secret.

There was only one other source for the information. The clinic must have called for some reason. Or perhaps a letter had been sent.

The bill. Of course. She'd forgotten all about the bill that would have arrived in the mail. McCord must have had the shock of his life when he opened it.

Shaking a little, this time from agitation, not nausea, Pru stood up and looked frantically around the room. The odds were he would have left the paperwork at home unless he'd arrived prepared to confront her with his knowledge.

McCord was always prepared. He would have brought the bill with him as proof in case she attempted to deny her pregnancy. Pru rushed across the room and flung open the closet door. She heard the shower pounding in the distance as she quickly went through the pockets of McCord's lightweight sport coat. Then she knelt to unzip the battered leather flight bag that McCord always used when he traveled.

Inside the bag she found fresh underwear, fresh shirts, a couple of silk ties and a buff-colored envelope bearing the return address of a women's health clinic in San Diego.

She straightened slowly, clutching the envelope in her hand as the door to the bathroom opened. She turned to see McCord standing in the doorway with a towel wrapped around his waist. He was watching her with those fathomless dark eyes.

"What's the matter now, Pru?"

Her fingers clenched around the envelope. "You knew, didn't you? You found out I was pregnant. That's why you insisted on marrying me. *You knew.*"

5

"I KNEW," McCord said very quietly.

"Damn it, why didn't you say anything?" Pru wailed.

"Why didn't *you* say anything," he countered.

"I didn't want you to marry me just because I was pregnant!"

"Oh, hell," McCord said grimly. "I should have guessed. I wondered why you didn't tell me. I thought maybe you were just too proud to use the baby to get what you wanted." He frowned. "Come to think of it, I guess that was part of the reason, wasn't it?"

She ignored his logic. "How could you do this to me, McCord? You've ruined everything." Pru felt her shaky emotions slipping out of control. She threw the incriminating envelope toward the trash container. It missed and fluttered lightly to the rug.

McCord folded his arms and lounged against the doorframe. He was good at that, Pru thought resentfully. On the rare occasions they had got involved in a serious argument, he'd usually spent a lot of the time propped in a doorway watching her with those bottomless dark eyes.

"You're getting emotional, Pru. I suppose that's only natural, given your present condition, but I think you'd better calm down and take a rational look at the situation."

"A rational look?" she stormed. "Meaning my aunt was right? I should just shut up and be grateful you decided to marry me? Well, I've got news for both of you. I'm not my mother. I'm not some dirt-poor small-town girl who thinks the only way to escape poverty is by getting some man to marry her. I'm not poor, remember? I have a good education, my own car, money in the bank and excellent job prospects. What's more, I'm living in sunny California where anything goes. I won't be shunned or ostracized. I can afford to have this baby and raise it alone. Lots of women are doing it these days."

"But you're not going to have this baby and raise it alone, are you, Pru? You're married now." McCord's gaze went deliberately to the region of her stomach and then lifted back to her face. "I'm the father of your child. If I hadn't come after you, you would never have told me, would you? Why not, Pru? Afraid that if I knew you were pregnant, I'd throw you out or demand that you get an abortion?"

She stared at him in shock. It was the coldness of his voice that startled her more than the words. Never in all the months she'd known him had he sounded quite this chilled and remote. "Of course not. I was afraid you'd probably marry me if you found out I was pregnant. That's why I didn't tell you. Can't you understand?"

He came away from the door, moving toward her with long, pacing strides. Pru tried to step back, but there was no place to retreat. The closet was directly behind her. When his hands closed over her shoulders, she flinched, not because he had hurt her, but because of the expression in his eyes.

"No, I don't understand," he stated through set teeth. "You wanted to get married. If you thought I'd marry you if I knew you were pregnant, *why didn't you use that as a weapon to get what you wanted?* Tell me, Pru. That's the one thing I haven't been able to figure out."

"Forcing you to marry me because of the baby is hardly a solid foundation on which to build a marriage." Pru moved one hand in a helpless little gesture. "I gave you my ultimatum, as you called it, because I thought it might bring you to your senses and make you see that what we had was good enough to warrant a...a more permanent arrangement. I thought if I could just shake you out of your state of smug, male satisfaction, you'd realize you really did want me. When you followed me to Annie's in Pasadena, I just assumed you'd finally come to the right conclusion about us and that you had decided you wanted to marry me after all."

He gave her a small shake. "Pru, listen to me, I did want to marry you."

"Because you found out I was pregnant."

"I won't deny that was a factor, but I would have come after you even if that bill hadn't arrived from the clinic."

She glared up at him. "Just answer one question, McCord."

His mouth tightened ominously. "What question?"

"Did the clinic bill arrive before or after you made up your mind to follow me to Pasadena?"

There was a short pause that gave Pru her answer before McCord even opened his mouth. She gave a resigned sigh as he said carefully, "Pru, the clinic bill came in the mail the day after you left. I was still in a rage because you'd dared to walk out on me."

She nodded her head forlornly, accepting the unalterable fact. "So it was knowing that I was pregnant that made you decide to act. You showed up in Pasadena a few days after that. Took you a while to figure out where I'd gone, I suppose."

"Yes, it did, damn it. I finally had to force J.P. to give me your personnel file. You never bothered to tell me your sister lived in Pasadena. You barely even mentioned that you had a sister. Come to think of it, you barely mentioned your Aunt Wilhelmina in Texas, either. It wasn't easy locating you. Why didn't you tell me more about your family, Pru?"

She tried a small shrug. It wasn't easy because he was still gripping her shoulders. "Why didn't you ever tell me about yours? Let's face it, McCord. Married people share information on families. Couples involved in a convenient no-strings-attached affair don't have any reason to discuss such things."

"I don't know why not. We talked about everything else under the sun." He released her and stalked across the room to the window. "You didn't make any effort to involve me with your family because you were embarrassed about the fact that you were living with me. That's it, isn't it, Pru?"

"Be grateful," she muttered. "Aunt Wilhelmina would have been down on you like a pile of rocks if she knew I was living with you."

"And your sister?"

"I told her when I moved in with you. She understood," Pru said quietly.

"But she didn't approve?"

"She worried about me. I think she thought I was taking a risk."

"And when you showed up pregnant and alone on her doorstep, she knew for certain you'd been taking a risk." McCord glanced back over his shoulder, his eyes hard.

Pru walked slowly over to the bed and sank down on it with her back to McCord. "I should have taken better precautions. I should have been more careful."

There was silence behind her and then McCord said quietly, "It was my fault. It happened that night I got back from Africa, didn't it?"

Pru nodded. "Yes."

He rubbed the back of his neck with a reflective, massaging action, as though trying to ease some inner tension. "I've never been so exhausted and angry and depressed in my life as I was the night I got back from that trip. I'd never seen such endless, unrelenting death. It's overwhelming. Trying to believe in a future for those people is almost impossible. Everything the foundation is trying to do represents such a small amount of assistance compared to what the land and nature and the various governments are doing to the people trying to stay alive."

"I understand," Pru said softly, hearing the depths of the carefully concealed emotion in his voice.

"When I woke up in the middle of the night and realized I was home and that you were with me, I didn't stop to think about taking precautions. All I wanted to do was confirm the fact that we were both still alive and that there was a future. The next morning I thought about how careless I had been. Then I forgot about it because you never said anything. I figured everything must be all right. It never occurred to me that you'd keep quiet if you discovered you were pregnant."

He didn't have to spell it out, she thought. She knew how that trip to Africa had affected him. When he'd awakened in the middle of the night, she hadn't given much thought to precautions, either. All her womanly instincts had been to offer comfort and warmth and confirmation of life.

For the first time since she'd awakened that morning, a small dart of wry amusement went through her. "I guess we got fairly irrefutable evidence of just how determined life is to go on," she murmured.

She sensed that her brief burst of humor had startled him. He came back from the window and sat down on the bed beside her. Pru felt the strength of his arm as he put it around her shoulder.

"I know this isn't starting out like the fairy-tale marriage you probably always wanted, Pru," McCord said quietly. "It's easy to see that I'm not exactly your idea of a knight in shining armor. But we're going to make things work. I told you last night that we've both made promises and a commitment."

"And now we're stuck with those promises and the commitment?" she challenged.

"You know the answer to that." His gaze was watchful and shadowed as he studied her face.

Pru thought of how much she loved this man and then she thought about the baby she was carrying. The child had a right to know his or her father, especially since the father was determined to shoulder his responsibilities. Slowly and deliberately Pru took hold of her frazzled emotions. McCord was right, of course. He usually was when it came to the practical, rational side of life.

"Under the circumstances, marriage appears to be the best option," she finally said very formally.

"It's the only option and we've already exercised it. There's no going back."

She smiled wearily. "You don't have to beat me over the head with it any longer. I was feeling a little emotional earlier, but I'm back under control now."

"I'm glad to hear it." He didn't look as though he quite believed her, however.

"I suppose," Pru continued thoughtfully, "that Aunt Wilhelmina is right. I really should be grateful to you for tracking me down and demanding marriage. A lot of men wouldn't have bothered."

His jaw hardened. "Damn it, Pru, I don't want your gratitude. We created this situation together and we'll work through it together."

Her mouth curved slightly as she slid out from under the shelter of his arm and got to her feet. "You mean I don't have to grovel three times a day and kiss your toes on Fridays?"

He stood up beside her, his hands moving possessively around the nape of her neck. "You can kiss my toes," he said deliberately, "any time you feel like it."

"Be still my beating heart." She wrinkled her nose. "I'm not sure that kind of excitement is good for the baby."

His eyes softened, and he pulled her close, burying his face in her hair. "It's going to be all right, honey. Everything's going to work out just fine. We may have got off to a somewhat rocky start, but the going will get smoother once we make up our minds to stop snapping at each other."

"You mean once I make up my mind to stop snapping at you, don't you, McCord? The truth is, you've been very good-natured and generous about this whole thing right from the start. I see that now. Earlier I was being selfish and emotional. It won't happen again."

He looked down into her earnest face and smiled faintly. "Is that right?"

She nodded determinedly. "Yes, it is. Don't laugh at me, McCord. I've been through enough lately. I don't need you laughing at me."

He groaned and squeezed her gently. "I'm not laughing at you, sweetheart." Her soft breasts were crushed against his chest, and a curling tendril of her hair wrapped itself around the hard muscle of his upper arm. "I'm just relieved there's not going to be any more argument on the subject of our marriage."

"I rarely argue with you, McCord."

"I know. But when you do, I feel like I'm in the middle of a lightning storm. You're unpredictable. I don't know which way to move for fear of provoking you further."

"That doesn't seem to stop you from trying to respond," she observed dryly.

"A man's got to do something when his woman's going up in flames." He started to lower his head so that he could kiss her, but she slipped out of his arms. "Pru?"

"It's getting late. I'd better take my shower." She was already walking into the bathroom. The satiny nightgown flowed around her slim ankles. "My appetite seems to be returning with a vengeance. I can't wait for breakfast. I'll be out in a few minutes, McCord."

The door slammed shut with some force. McCord stood looking at it for a long, thoughtful moment. He wanted to believe the resolute edict he'd just handed down to his new wife. He wanted to convince himself that everything really was straightened out and that there would be smooth sailing from now on between them.

But there was no point trying to kid himself. Pru had accepted the marriage, but she wasn't truly happy or content with her situation. She'd wanted to be married for what she thought of as all the right reasons. Instead, she was convinced McCord had married her out of a sense of duty and responsibility.

He didn't have any means of proving otherwise.

McCord spent some time dwelling on the irony of her conclusions. She assumed he had married her because he felt responsible for the baby. He wondered what his family would think if they knew how firmly she believed her own analysis of his actions. It made an amusing picture.

He pushed the thought aside as he walked to the closet and pulled out his jeans and a long-sleeved white shirt. For the first time he gave serious consideration to how he had reacted when he'd seen the bill from the clinic. It would have been nice if he could have at least offered Pru the reassurance of knowing he'd already made up his mind to come after her before the bill arrived.

But the truth was, he'd been both outraged and enraged the day following her departure. He'd felt betrayed in a way he'd never experienced before in his life, not even after he'd discovered three years ago that Laura Reynolds, his fiancée, was pregnant. The emotions that had been eating at him since the moment Pru had walked out the door had been unnerving and frightening in their intensity.

He'd spent some time assuring himself Pru would come crawling back on her hands and knees. He'd even fantasized about how he would react when she did. His fantasies had been greatly aided by the large quantity of whiskey he'd consumed after J.P.'s interminable, boring dinner party had finally ended. Such parties were always a bore when Pru wasn't around to manage things. She had a knack for putting people at ease and keeping a conversation going. As J.P. was fond of saying, people responded to Pru the way flies did to potato salad.

The fantasies he'd concocted the night after the party and had perfected while dawn broke over the California coast were brilliantly, satisfyingly vivid. In his mind he'd worked out an elaborate reconciliation scene in which Pru would cry and apologize and promise never to leave again.

He, on the other hand, would have been remote and distant at first, then politely condescending, and finally, generously forgiving. The little scene had quite naturally ended with a vision of taking Pru to bed where she could properly make up for all she'd put him through.

Before he'd worked out all the details of his fantasy, the morning mail had arrived, bringing with it the bill from the clinic. The moment he'd opened it, everything had changed.

No, that wasn't true. Nothing had changed. McCord fastened the snaps of his jeans with a brisk, savage efficiency. The end result was the same. One way or another he would have found a means of bringing

Pru back where she belonged. Her place, whether she knew it or not, was in his home and in his bed.

PRU WAS AMAZED by her own hunger at breakfast. She wolfed down four slices of whole wheat toast, two poached eggs, a pile of hash browns and a large glass of orange juice before she even realized what she was doing. As she polished off the last of the toast, she saw McCord watching her with amusement in his eyes. She flushed and put down the scrap of toast, uneaten.

"If I'm not careful, I'm going to gain a ton," she muttered.

He picked up the bit of toast and held it to her lips. "Don't worry about it. You're going to look cute plump."

"Thanks a lot," she said, annoyed. But as soon as she opened her mouth he pushed the toast inside, and she had no other recourse except to eat it. It tasted delicious. She could have eaten three more slices, but she was careful not to say so. "Are we going back to La Jolla today?"

McCord hesitated and then shook his head. "No."

Pru glanced around at the elegant dining room. "You want to stay here longer?" She wasn't sure how she felt about that. Her feeling of being on a real honeymoon had ended this morning when she'd found the clinic envelope.

"I'd like to stay here a while longer," McCord said, watching her closely, "but we can come back another time. We should be heading back to La Jolla as soon as possible, but there's something I want to do first."

Pru nodded, realizing she wanted to return home. It was strange how she'd thought of McCord's house as her home from the moment she'd moved in with him. "Fine." There was no disguising the sense of relief she felt. The honeymoon was definitely over. It had been over before it had begun.

McCord saw her reaction, and his dark brows came together in a severe expression. "An overnight trip isn't much of a honeymoon."

Pru lifted one shoulder with studied negligence. "It's perfectly adequate under the circumstances."

He looked as if he wanted to argue, but he didn't. Instead, he said calmly, "There's something we have to do before we go home."

She eyed him inquiringly. "So you said. What is it?"

He cradled his coffee cup in two hands and took a deep swallow. "I want to introduce you to my family."

Pru considered that. "You make it sound as though you'll be introducing me to the Spanish Inquisition. Have you got a bunch of Aunt Wilhelminas in your family?"

"Believe me," McCord said bluntly, "Aunt Wilhelmina is a pussycat compared to my relatives. At least your aunt never actually disinherited you and informed you she thought you were dishonorable, disloyal and disgusting."

"I'm not sure I like the alliteration. That's a lot of dises. Disinherited, dishonorable, disloyal and disgusting." Pru was amazed. "What kind of family have you got, anyway?"

"A very proud, very stubborn, very unforgiving one. Also, a very wealthy one. My father made his money early on in California real estate. I grew up on a farm that just happened to be in the middle of Orange County. Twenty years ago my father sold the land to real estate developers for a fortune. My father is a very shrewd man. As it happened, he had a natural flair for making money with land. He converted the profits from the farm into a very successful real estate development company, which promptly invested in more land. After that, there was no stopping him. Officially he's still president of McCord Enterprises, but he's turned the day-to-day running of the operation over to my younger brother, Kyle. Kyle is shaping up to be even shrewder and more successful than my father. McCord Enterprises is growing by leaps and bounds."

Pru's eyes widened. "Are both your parents alive?"

"Very much alive." McCord took another sip of coffee. "So is my brother Kyle and his wife Carrie. Kyle is doing the McCords proud."

The way he said that caught Pru's attention. "Was that supposed to be your job? Before you got, uh, disinherited?"

"I'm the oldest son," McCord said without any inflection. "My father always assumed I'd step into his shoes. Even after I insisted on majoring in agricultural sciences, he still had hopes. I . . . tried to please him for a few years."

Pru tipped her head to one side and tapped one fingernail lightly on the tablecloth. "Lucky for you, you got kicked out of the family fold, hmm?"

It was McCord's turn to look surprised. "Why do you say that?"

"It saved you from having to become a full-time corporate executive and follow in your father's footsteps. I can't imagine a worse fate for you, McCord. You need to be able to deal with more fundamental things." She smiled faintly. "You're a farmer at heart. It's hard enough for you and J.P. to do the kind of socializing and entertaining required for Arlington Foundation business as it is. I can't imagine you trapped behind a desk all day, too. If you'd taken over the reins of your dad's firm, you would have been stuck in a fancy corporate office. The closest you would have got to the land was going out on a golf course."

McCord continued to stare at her for a long moment and then a slow grin appeared on his face. "You're right, you know. It would have been a disaster. I didn't realize it myself until after I was banished."

"Were you actually banished, McCord?"

"Not officially. My parents just made it clear I was a grave disappointment to them and unworthy of my name and heritage. I seem to recall saying something at the time to the effect that people who had been growing beans for a living less than twenty years ago didn't have to be overly concerned about names and heritages. The argument deteriorated rapidly after that. It ended with me walking out of their lives. I took the Ferrari and what I had in the bank and that was it."

"What on earth did you do to alienate your family so completely?" Pru couldn't imagine any father being less than proud of a son like Case McCord.

"It's a long, dull story, Pru." McCord withdrew emotionally from the conversation. It was as though a shutter had been lowered to conceal his eyes. Once again they were dark and fathomless. "Let's just say I didn't marry the right woman."

Pru's mouth fell open in shock. "You were supposed to marry a certain woman?" she asked weakly.

"It was three years ago, Pru. I've already told you. She's dead now."

"The fiancée you mentioned the other night at dinner?" Pru asked tightly.

"That's right. Her father was my father's best friend and a partner in many of his deals. Laura was supposed to inherit a fair-sized chunk of McCord Enterprises. Shortly before he died, her father asked my father to look after Laura. My parents thought of her as the daughter they never had. Laura's mother disappeared years ago after a divorce, so when her dad died the McCords became her family. As it happened, everyone thought Laura and I made a good couple."

"Including you and Laura?" Her breath felt trapped in her chest, Pru thought. Consciously she tried to release the tension that had gripped her.

"Yes," McCord said. "Including Laura and me. She was a beautiful blond angel. Everyone loved her. And she said she loved me."

"Oh." Pru couldn't think of anything to say to that.

"Yes, oh."

"Well?" Pru finally prompted. "What happened?"

McCord looked into his coffee. "I changed my mind about the engagement. I decided I didn't want to marry her. When I told her, she went into a rage. She was almost hysterical. I didn't dare leave her alone that night until she'd calmed down somewhat. I didn't leave her apartment until nearly two in the morning when she finally settled down long enough to throw me out. I left. But almost as soon as I was gone she jumped into a car and went tearing off into the night. The police said she must have been going nearly a hundred miles an hour when she lost control on the freeway."

"Oh, my God," Pru breathed.

McCord's eyes hardened. "She died three hours later at the hospital. My family was gathered around the bedside. It was a very dramatic scene, I assure you. Laura regained consciousness long enough to inform everyone present exactly why she had been roaring along a Los Angeles freeway at close to a hundred miles an hour at two-thirty in the morning."

"She blamed you?" Pru asked, shocked.

McCord nodded. "You might say I was condemned by a dying woman's words. It was a tough act to follow, believe me." He didn't say anything else.

"How awful. What a terrible mess. But didn't your family understand that, while it was a tragedy, it was hardly your fault?"

"No. There were..." He paused, clearly searching for the right word. "Extenuating circumstances, I guess you could say."

"What extenuating circumstances?"

"They don't matter anymore, Pru. It was all over three years ago. The final conclusion was that I really should have married Laura. I had led her on and allowed her to believe she would be my wife. When I cold-bloodedly bowed out of the arrangement, she was distraught. Laura had a very delicate temperament."

McCord had obviously decided he'd said enough on the subject. Pru knew him better than to press for more information at that point. In fact, she was surprised at the amount he'd given her. In the past fifteen minutes she'd learned more about McCord's past and his family than she'd learned in the previous six months. "So the net result was that your father decided your brother was a more worthy son and made him CEO of the company?"

"Something like that. It sounds simple enough now, doesn't it? At the time it seemed damned messy."

"Have you seen much of your parents or your brother and his wife during the past three years?"

"Two years ago I spent Christmas Day with them. It was an awkward occasion for all concerned, to put it mildly. I didn't try to duplicate the experience."

"But now you've decided to introduce me to the family?" Pru asked uneasily.

"It won't be pleasant, but no one's going to attack you, Pru. It's me they blame for the situation. We won't stay long, I promise. I just want to make sure they know who you are and that you're my wife. After all, when the baby comes, they'll have to know about it."

"The baby?" she whispered. "Do we have to tell them about the baby right away? Couldn't we wait?"

"Why do you want to wait?" McCord asked, his eyes narrowing.

Pru groped for reasons she couldn't put into words. "It's too soon. I'm still adjusting to the fact that I'm pregnant. Give me a little time, McCord."

"Nothing's going to change with time," he pointed out gently. "You'll just be more and more pregnant."

"It's not funny," she retorted, seeing the flare of amusement in his eyes.

"I know. I shouldn't tease you. I realize you've been through a lot during the past few weeks. Now I'm asking you to face a pack of in-laws I'm not especially fond of myself. I won't add to the strain by announcing that not only did we get married yesterday, but you're already pregnant."

"Thank you, McCord," she said politely.

"You're embarrassed, aren't you?" he demanded with unexpected masculine insight. "That's the real reason you don't want me to mention that you're pregnant. You don't want everyone thinking you had to get married."

Pru bit her lip. She wasn't sure of her own reasons. She just knew she felt pressured and stressed and all sorts of other emotions that were probably common to mothers-to-be. "I'd just as soon not say anything yet," she murmured stubbornly.

"If you think it's going to be awkward having people think you had to get married because you were pregnant, how the hell did you plan to handle being an unwed mother?"

"That was different."

"How was it different?"

"I can't explain, and I'm sick of trying. Let's just drop the subject. I will announce my pregnancy in my own good time," she flared. It was all wrapped up in knowing she hadn't been married for the right reasons, all bound up with the knowledge that McCord had only married her because he was the kind of man who shouldered his responsibilities. She had been married for all the wrong reasons. She needed time to accept that.

McCord shook his head, half impatient and half sympathetic. "Women," he growled.

"Men," Pru growled back.

6

PRU HAD REGAINED a grip on her volatile emotions by the time McCord had the Ferrari packed. She told herself repeatedly she had absolutely no cause for complaint about her situation. She should be downright grateful, in fact, just as Aunt Wilhelmina had advised. Pru knew only too well that many women in similar circumstances would have found themselves on their own. She was lucky enough to be married to the baby's father. She had no grounds for carping about her fate.

But she was feeling perverse.

McCord installed Pru in the passenger seat of the Ferrari and then climbed into the driver's side. He shot Pru a quick, questioning glance as he turned the key in the ignition.

"Are you all right?"

"I'm fine."

"You have an odd look on your face. What are you thinking about?"

Pru deliberately grimaced, making her expression even odder. "I was just giving myself a pep talk."

"About what?" he demanded, guiding the car out of the inn parking lot.

"About not complaining when there is nothing to really complain about," she snapped, feeling goaded.

"You've decided to start feeling grateful instead?"

She didn't like the tone of his voice. "I don't intend to go overboard with it, but, yes, I guess I should be feeling rather grateful."

"I've told you I don't want your gratitude," he said.

"You'd rather have me throwing tantrums and railing against my fate?" she countered.

"As J.P. would say, some folks would complain if they got hung with a new rope."

"That sounds suspiciously like an Aunt Wilhelmina saying. And I am not complaining. I told you, I'm practicing being grateful."

"How about we just drop the subject?"

Pru slanted him a sideways glance and discovered he was making an effort to hang on to his temper. She could always tell when McCord was angry. His jaw became rigid with the force of his restrained emotions. "That might be best," she agreed softly, and turned her attention to the passing scenery.

The sparkling Pacific Ocean stretched to the horizon on the left-hand side of the Ferrari. The morning fog that frequently clouded the coastline in summer had burned off. It would be a warm day.

"Where do your parents live?" Pru asked after thirty minutes of silence.

"They have a place outside of Santa Barbara." McCord's tone was neutral.

"Where's the corporation based?"

"L.A."

"And your brother and his wife? Do they live in Los Angeles?"

"Marina del Rey," McCord said briefly, naming one of the posh oceanfront communities that comprised part of the Los Angeles sprawl.

"Are your parents expecting us?"

"I phoned my mother yesterday and told her we'd be arriving this afternoon. We'll only stay an hour or two, Pru. We should be able to survive that long."

"By then your filial duty will have been done, is that it? You will have introduced your new bride to your family, and that's all that's required under the circumstances?"

"That's all," he confirmed flatly. "I'm not taking you to meet them out of a sense of duty, though."

"Why, then?" She was genuinely curious.

"I'm not sure," he said with surprising honesty. "I think it's got something to do with the fact that I want them to know the family line is continuing through me, whether they approve or not. I want them to be aware of you."

Pru thought for a moment. "Was your mother shocked to hear that you'd married?" she finally asked in a rather tentative voice.

"Very."

Pru groaned silently, wondering what kind of welcome awaited her. "Then I'm definitely glad we've decided to wait to tell them about the baby. I don't want to be responsible for giving your mother too many shocks at once."

THE HOME OF MCCORD'S PARENTS was an imposing modern structure set high above the sea and commanding views of both ocean and rolling hills. Pru was a little startled at the size and grandeur of it. For the first time she began to realize just how wealthy the senior McCords were. Pru eyed the sleek, modern, heavily glassed structure as McCord turned the Ferrari into the long, winding drive.

"Were you raised in this house?" she asked, suddenly and intensely curious. "After you left the farm?"

"No. My parents had this place built a few years ago. They used it as a vacation home until my father retired from running McCord Enterprises. They live here full-time now."

"It's quite impressive." Pru couldn't think of anything else to say.

"Do you like it?"

"Nice place to visit, but I wouldn't want to live here," she returned promptly.

He laughed. "Why not?"

"I like our home better."

He flicked her a glance at the words "our home," but he said nothing.

Pru didn't notice the glance. She wasn't paying any attention to him now as he parked the car in the drive. The wide, elegantly proportioned double doors of the house had opened, revealing an attractive woman who must have been nearly sixty but who appeared to be at least ten years younger. Her hair was toned to a rich California blond shade and styled in a short, upswept manner that accented her large, expressive eyes. The beautifully cut khaki slacks and cream-colored blouse that she wore spelled money in a very smooth, understated way.

"Your mother?" Pru asked.

McCord switched off the ignition and stared at the figure on the doorstep. "Her name is Evelyn."

Evelyn McCord came down the steps. As the older woman drew closer, Pru saw the tension and anxiety that couldn't quite be concealed by the bright, welcoming smile. McCord's mother was far more tense about this meeting than Pru was. Nevertheless, Pru held her breath as McCord climbed out of the car and accepted his mother's greeting. It consisted of a very restrained kiss on the cheek. Neither party made any effort to prolong the physical contact.

Pru climbed slowly out of the car as both McCord and his mother turned toward her. It was when Evelyn's hazel gaze met that of her new daughter-in-law that Pru saw there was more than tension in the depths of her eyes. There was a spark of something Pru could have sworn was hope.

The introductions were quickly made. Pru smiled at Evelyn and held out her hand.

"I'm so pleased to meet you," Evelyn said swiftly, rapidly assessing Pru's face. "It was such a surprise to hear from Case yesterday. I had no idea ... That is we didn't dream he was engaged, much less married. Do come inside and meet Hale. Case, why don't you bring in the luggage? You can put it in the west bedroom. It has a lovely view."

"There's no need for me to bring in the luggage, Mother. Pru and I are only going to stay for an hour or so. I just brought her by to meet you and Dad."

Pru winced at the cold, curt refusal. She saw a well-concealed despair replace the flickering hope that had been in Evelyn McCord's eyes.

"Oh, dear," Evelyn said unhappily. "I was so hoping you could stay the night at least. It's been so long. I've invited your brother and his wife for dinner. We're hoping Devin Blanchard can make it, too. They'll be staying overnight and going back to L.A. in the morning."

McCord shot his mother an unreadable glance. "You invited Kyle and Carrie and Devin?"

Evelyn flinched as if he'd made an accusation. Then her mouth firmed. "I thought it only right that they meet your new wife, Case."

Before McCord could respond a man's voice spoke from the doorway. "The least you could do under the circumstances is stay for dinner. Your mother's gone to a lot of work, Case."

Pru turned to see an older version of Case standing on the threshold of the house. His dark hair was nearly silvered, but the brilliant, dark gaze was as intent and shadowed and proud as that of his son. His face was as fiercely carved, and the underlying masculine arrogance was unmistakable. Hale McCord was still a strong, well-built man although he carried more weight than did his son. Pru would have guessed instantly who he was, even if she hadn't known his name. Now she knew where Case McCord had gotten his pride and his arrogance and his sheer, cussed stubbornness.

"Hello, Dad. I'd like you to meet my wife, Prudence," McCord said coolly. "Pru, in case you haven't guessed, this is my father, Hale McCord." He turned back to face his parent. "I'm sorry about Mother's plans, but I told her yesterday when I called that we wouldn't be here long."

Evelyn looked at him with a pleading expression. "Couldn't you at least stay for dinner, Case? It's been so long." Helplessly she shifted her glance to Pru.

Pru couldn't stand the pain in the woman's eyes. She smiled at Evelyn and moved forward to take her husband's arm. "There's no reason at all why we can't stay for dinner, is there, McCord? In fact, we can spend the night. We'd love to. We don't have to be back in La Jolla until tomorrow or the next day."

"Pru," McCord began grimly, "there's no need to spend anymore than an hour here."

"Nonsense," Pru countered firmly. "This is a beautiful spot, and I would love to spend the night." She felt the tension in McCord's arm and widened her smile. She turned the full force of it on Evelyn McCord. "Thank you very much for the invitation, Mrs. McCord. It's wonderful of you to have us on such short notice."

"Please, call me Evelyn." The rush of maternal gratitude was almost embarrassing.

"Damn it, Pru . . ." McCord's voice was a low snarl of anger.

Pru released him and started up the steps with a hand extended toward her new father-in-law. "Bring in the luggage, McCord," she ordered casually over her shoulder, silently praying she would get away with the command. "How do you do, Mr. McCord? I would have known you anywhere. I'll bet you were raised on a farm, too. Does wonders for a man's shoulders."

Hale McCord blinked at her as if not knowing quite how to take the outrageous flattery. Then he seemed to decide it was safe to respond to the amusement in Pru's eyes. He accepted her hand in his large paw. "You're right, Prudence. I spent a lot of years picking beans and bailing hay. Who do you think taught Case how to do those things? Call me Hale."

"Call me Pru. Everyone else does." She risked a quick glance back toward the car and gave an inward sigh of relief when she saw that McCord was lifting the luggage out of the Ferrari.

Evelyn's eyes were darting anxiously from the luggage to Pru as if she didn't quite dare to believe her son had agreed to stay the night. When Pru smiled reassuringly at her from the top of the steps, she returned the expression with genuine warmth and came forward quickly. She apparently decided her luck was going to hold. She came up the steps to urge Pru inside the hall.

"Thank you, my dear," she murmured in such a low tone that only Pru heard her. "Thank you very much. I'm in your debt." Then she raised her voice. "Come along and I'll show you your bedroom. Hale, why don't you give Case a hand with the luggage?"

Hale looked toward the Ferrari, as if not quite certain how to handle the simple offer of assistance. Then he nodded abruptly and started down the steps.

"Here, Case. I'll take one of those bags," Hale said brusquely.

"It's all right, Dad, I've got them."

"I said I'll take one, damn it."

Without a word McCord surrendered one of the bags to his father, who turned around and stalked back into the house.

Pru felt the shudder of dismay in the woman beside her and wanted to put her arm around her in sympathy. *My God*, she thought, *what a family. They're all dancing on eggs and juggling dynamite, as Aunt Wilhelmina would say.* At least Aunt Wilhelmina was up front and vocal about her feelings. She didn't try to hide behind this unnerving, barely polite facade.

A young woman appeared in the hall, smiling inquiringly.

"This is Sandra," Evelyn explained. "She helps out around here. She's already got your room made up. Sandra, this is my son's new wife, Prudence."

"How do you do?" Sandra said politely. "Let me know if you need anything."

"Thanks," Pru murmured.

"Here we are, Pru. Hale, you can set the suitcase down over there." Evelyn bustled around the elegant salmon-and-gray bedroom, straightening the already perfectly straight bedspread and flicking an infinitesimally small bit of lint off the sleek lacquer dresser. She glanced anxiously at Pru. "Will this room be all right, Pru?"

Once again Pru felt compelled to summon a brilliantly reassuring smile. "It's fantastic. What a beautiful view. I won't be able to sleep tonight. I'll spend the whole time looking out the window. It's amazing how different the ocean looks from one portion of the coast to another, isn't it? The view from McCord's, I mean *our* home, is completely different."

There was a fraught moment of silence while Evelyn glanced past Pru to her son's set face. "I wouldn't know," she murmured. "I've never visited Case in La Jolla."

McCord said nothing. He set the luggage down and walked over to the window as if he were mildly curious about the view. Hale shifted awkwardly in the doorway. Evelyn bit her lip.

Pru swallowed another silent groan of dismay and prayed she'd be able to keep her foot out of her mouth for the rest of the afternoon and evening. She plowed on with dogged determination. "What time will McCord's brother Kyle and his wife get here? I'm anxious to meet them."

"They should be here by five, don't you think, Hale?" Evelyn jumped to take advantage of the neutral conversational opening.

"Sure. Somewhere around five," Hale muttered.

"Well," Evelyn went on with patently false cheerfulness, "why don't you two freshen up? When you're done perhaps you'd like to take a walk down on the beach."

"That sounds wonderful," Pru assured her. She almost collapsed in relief when the bedroom door closed behind McCord's parents. She sank down on the bed and watched her husband's broad-shouldered back.

"It's going to be a hell of an evening," McCord said.

"I can see that."

"Just remember," he advised with a sardonic twist of his mouth as he swung around to face her, "that it's all your fault. I was a fool to let you push me into agreeing to stay. I wish you joy of your new in-laws, Pru." He stalked into the adjoining bathroom and slammed the door.

Pru didn't realize just how bad matters were going to get until Kyle and Carrie McCord arrived shortly before five o'clock. Things might have been tense around McCord's parents, but Pru didn't encounter real hostility until she confronted Carrie McCord.

Kyle and his wife were a handsome couple. Kyle shared his father's dark eyes and thick hair, but he lacked the muscular build of his parent and his brother. Instead, he was slim and dynamic, with a clean-cut, well-dressed, California executive manner.

Carrie was a lovely blue-eyed redhead. Under normal circumstances, Pru was certain her new sister-in-law would have been slender and well proportioned. Carrie was, however, quite pregnant. Her designer maternity dress shaped a body that had to be very close to nine months along.

Pru experienced a sudden urge to confide her own pregnant status to Carrie. She found herself abruptly eager to compare notes and ask questions. But the urge disintegrated at once when she saw the anger and resentment in Carrie's blue eyes. The other woman was superficially polite, but there was no welcome for the new member of the family.

She hates me, Pru thought in shock. *I don't even know her and already she hates me*. It was hard to believe that all the anger and tension in this family had been generated by a dying woman's accusation three years ago. There had to be more to the story, and Pru wondered desperately what it might be. It was obvious no one intended to talk about the subject.

"Devin Blanchard decided at the last moment he could come for the evening, Mom," Kyle McCord told his mother as he quietly greeted his brother and prepared to remove luggage from the BMW he drove. "He should be here any minute."

"Wonderful," Evelyn said quickly, casting another anxious glance at her oldest son. "I'm so glad he could make it. You and Devin used to be such good friends, didn't you, Case? I'm sure you'll enjoy seeing him again. Let's go inside. Hale was just about to pour drinks."

Everyone seemed grateful for the small social ritual of the predinner cocktail hour. No one questioned Pru when she seconded Carrie's order of fruit juice. Hale handed out the drinks, and Evelyn and Pru gamely tried to keep the conversation going until the sound of another car was heard in the drive.

"That'll be Dev," Carrie said. She shot McCord an odd look. "You haven't seen him for quite some time, have you, Case? Let's see, the last time would have been three years ago when Laura died."

Pru couldn't believe her sister-in-law had had the gall to introduce the dead woman's name into the conversation. It was so painfully obvious that everyone else was desperately trying to avoid any reference to what had happened three years ago.

McCord merely shrugged and took a swallow of his whiskey. "No. I haven't seen him since then."

"You and Devin worked together on a number of McCord projects," Evelyn said wistfully.

McCord gave her a grim smile. "Things change, don't they?"

Evelyn was saved from having to answer because Hale opened the door at that moment to the newcomer. Pru studied Devin Blanchard curiously.

He was a sandy-haired, green-eyed man who appeared to be about McCord's age. Dressed in an expensive casual linen sport coat and slacks that had a European cut, he was handsome with the kind of sensitive yet rugged look that appealed to women. When he shook hands with Pru, he gave her a warm smile.

"Congratulations on finally trapping him, Pru," Devin said in an easy, bantering tone. "The last time I talked to Case about marriage, he had sworn off it for life."

Pru winced inwardly at the words, but she was so relieved to have someone speak in a normal, friendly tone of voice that she immediately forgave Devin. "It doesn't happen often, because he's a very stubborn man, but believe it or not, McCord does occasionally change his mind," she said lightly.

Devin grinned at her and then at McCord. "Nothing like a pretty woman to help convince a man he might have to reevaluate a decision. How are you doing, Case? It's been a long time."

"Fine, Dev. What about yourself?" McCord was polite, his voice utterly neutral, although he shook hands with the other man in a reasonably relaxed fashion.

"I'm doing great. Still working for Kyle."

"The board of directors made Dev a vice president three months ago," Kyle informed his brother. "He's become my right-hand man."

"Only because of your recommendation," Devin said, smiling.

Kyle shrugged. "It's about time you got paid for the amount of responsibility you're handling. You've always played a vital role in McCord Enterprises." He turned to Pru. "Devin has been with the company for several years. He and Case put together some major deals in their time. We're still making money on all of them."

"I see," Pru said politely.

"That was before Kyle took over the reins," Carrie put in with a militant gleam in her eye. "My husband has been running McCord Enterprises for the past three years. The projects Kyle has put together since Case left are considerably larger and more profitable than those earlier deals."

Pru heard the challenge behind the words and wondered at it. Then she remembered that it was Case

McCord who had been groomed originally to take over the running of the company. Kyle had got the job more or less by default when McCord and his father had quarreled three years ago.

Pru had a sudden insight into the probable cause of Carrie's overt hostility. It was quite possible Carrie was afraid that, having married at last, her brother-in-law might have decided to reclaim his lost heritage. Pru smiled at the other woman with genuine empathy.

"I understand Kyle is doing an excellent job managing McCord Enterprises," she said easily. "It's strange how things sometimes work out for the best, isn't it? It's quite obvious Kyle has a flair for corporate management and it's just as obvious that it would have been a mistake for McCord to have stayed in that role."

Everyone in the glass-walled living room stared at her. Even McCord eyed her with an unblinking gaze. But it was Hale who spoke.

"What makes you say that, Pru?"

"I've known McCord for several months now," Pru said gently, "and I can say for certain that he would have been very discontented sitting behind an executive's desk at McCord Enterprises. My husband's true talent is in coaxing the land to produce as much as it's capable of producing. That talent happens to be a very valuable one in certain places around the world where people are systematically starving to death. McCord belongs in the Arlington Foundation's experimental crop fields or in an open-air classroom teaching farmers new techniques. The only kind of office work he enjoys is putting together a research paper on soils or designing a plan to increase plant productivity. He'd be bored and restless playing corporate officer in a high-rise office building. J.P. says he's got the magic touch when it comes to figuring out how to turn a desert into an Eden."

Everyone was still staring at her. Carrie was watching Pru with a distinctly suspicious glare. Devin Blanchard seemed politely interested. Kyle was looking quizzical. McCord's parents appeared startled by Pru's words, and McCord himself had a familiar, amused expression on his face. It was Hale who responded first.

"Who's J.P.?" he asked.

"J. P. Arlington. He's the founder of the Arlington Foundation."

Evelyn nodded slowly. "Case did say something once on the phone about going to work for a foundation of some sort."

Good Lord, Pru thought, *these people barely even know where McCord lives, let alone what he's doing for a living.* Whatever rift had occurred in this family three years ago, it must have been the size of the Grand Canyon. Still, she had a conversational gambit now, and Pru wasn't about to let go. She hadn't been J.P.'s executive hostess for the past six months for nothing. She could handle a roomful of difficult, uneasy, occasionally hostile people.

Pru launched into a glowing report on the Arlington Foundation for Agricultural Research and Development. She hadn't just been J.P.'s hostess, she had also been the editor of the foundation's journal. When called upon Pru could give an excellent summary of the status of agriculture around the world and who was doing what about it.

To her amazement, she discovered that her audience seemed quite fascinated. They lacked the courage or the nerve to ask McCord what he had been doing for the past three years, but they seized on the opportunity of learning about him through his new wife.

McCord sat back in silence, his glass cradled in his hands, and watched Pru answer questions. Bringing her here had been akin to throwing some poor, unsuspecting nonswimmer into a pool and letting her figure out how to stay afloat. But Pru was learning fast, he thought with admiration. His family and Blanchard were responding the way people always did to her. Her talent for putting people at ease was extraordinary.

She had them all listening and talking now. Some of the tension had seeped out of the room. Even his father was asking genuinely interested questions about the foundation's work. His mother's relief at the nonhostile turn of events was embarrassingly evident.

In general, the reactions of his family were almost amusing. It was Devin Blanchard's intent attention to Pru's conversation that ruffled the latent possessive streak in McCord.

"Of course, Hale," Pru announced glibly, "I'm not saying that his agricultural background is all McCord draws upon in his work. The kind of things you must have taught him about running a large organization come in extremely handy. J.P. relies on McCord to deal with a lot of the management aspects of the foundation's work. There's a fair amount of travel involved, too. McCord has been all over the world in his work for the foundation."

"Case has a natural talent for leadership," Hale said with a reflective look at his son. "He always had a knack for being able to put together a team and get every member working toward a common goal."

"Well, I assure you, it's being put to good use at the foundation. You can't imagine how difficult it is to convince a bunch of poor, desperate farmers on the other side of the world to try a new agricultural technique. They're afraid to try anything new for fear of losing what little they've already got. And then, naturally, there's the business of dealing with various and assorted bureaucratic and academic types. McCord's got a way with those people, too. You're right. He can pull things together."

Carrie's gaze went to her brother-in-law. "You seem to have married a one-woman cheerleading squad, Case."

Pru flushed at the sarcasm, but McCord merely smiled enigmatically. "I'm lucky to have a wife who believes in me so completely," he said blandly. "Every man needs a woman who believes in him, doesn't he? Sometimes there's no one else in the world who does."

There was an appalled silence as everyone in the room appeared to take the remark personally.

"Quite a little treasure," Carrie muttered with a narrow glance at Pru.

Even her husband was somewhat embarrassed by Carrie's comment. He cleared his throat, as though trying to find a new topic of conversation.

McCord ignored his brother's efforts. Instead, he raised his glass in a small, intimate salute to Pru. "She is, indeed, a treasure. I hate to think of how close I was to letting her slip through my fingers."

Pru's embarrassed flush turned to a glowing warmth. She stared at her husband, who was silhouetted against a flaming sunset. His gaze was dark and deep and brilliant. In that moment it was quite easy to believe he meant what he had said.

PRU MANAGED TO AVOID Carrie until after dinner when she found herself alone with her sister-in-law for a few minutes shortly before everyone retired to bed. It had been a mistake to come out alone onto the deck for a breath of sea air. That much was obvious the moment Pru heard the other woman behind her. She didn't turn around. She had a hunch what was coming.

"Well, well, well," Carrie said coldly. "Getting a little tired from playing the role of Great Peacemaker for the McCord family?"

Pru leaned on the railing and gazed out over the night-shrouded sea. "This family could use some peace," she said quietly.

"This family was doing just fine until you entered the picture. How in the world did you trap McCord into marrying you? You don't look like his type."

"What is his type, Carrie?"

"Laura Reynolds was. Tall, blond, classically beautiful, stylish."

"And dead."

"Yes. And dead." Carrie came closer to the railing, her bulky figure moving a little awkwardly. "Has Case told you about her?"

"Yes."

"All of it?"

"Enough," Pru assured her quietly.

"Including the fact that he killed her?"

Pru spun around, incensed. "He did not kill her. That's a horrible thing to say. The woman killed herself in a hundred-mile-an-hour crash on a freeway. There is no one else to be blamed."

Carrie's eyes glittered. "That depends on how you look at it. You weren't around three years ago, Pru. The rest of us were. We know exactly what happened and who was to blame."

"That, as my Aunt Wilhelmina would say, is so much refried chicken manure. If you haven't figured that out by now, then you aren't noticeably brighter than the chickens that make the manure." Pru turned back to the railing.

"You don't fool me for one minute, Pru." Carrie's voice was a tight, angry hiss. "I know exactly why you're here. Case McCord would never have returned if you hadn't found some way of convincing him it might be possible to—" She broke off hastily.

"Possible to do what, Carrie?" But Pru was fairly certain she already knew.

"You think you can patch things up in this family and get Case back into Hale's good graces, don't you? You've found out just how much money and power this family has and you figure you deserve a slice of it because you married the eldest son. It must have come as a shock when you discovered you'd married the wrong son, hmm? You'd picked the black sheep in the family. The one who was kicked out without a penny. I'll bet he didn't mention that small fact before the marriage, did he? Now you're desperately trying to find a way to fix that little problem, aren't you? It must be terrible standing on the outside in the cold, looking in on all this money. But you're smart. You must know Evelyn would give her soul to bring Case back into the fold. So you're going to try to do just that."

"Carrie, you've got this all wrong."

"The hell I have. But I'll tell you one thing, Pru, you'd better live up to your name and exercise a little caution. Because I see right through you. I know what you're up to and I'm not going to let you do it. I won't let you find a way to get your husband put back in charge of McCord Enterprises. Kyle's been running things for three years. He's been brilliant at it. The corporation is richer now than it's ever been. He deserves to go on running the operation. I won't let you wreck everything he's built up during the past few years!"

Stunned, Pru stared after her distraught sister-in-law as Carrie hurried back into the glass-walled living room.

7

McCord LOUNGED in the gray leather chair near the bedroom window, waiting for Pru to emerge from the bathroom. He sat in shadow, naked except for his jeans, which he'd left unsnapped. The only light in the gray-and-salmon room was the crack of yellow that seeped out from under the bathroom door.

The house was quiet now, but it seemed to him that underlying tension still thickened the air. It was as if the place had absorbed the emotions of its occupants while they were awake and was now releasing the essence of their uncertainties, hostility and stubborn pride back into the atmosphere around them.

There should be something more mixed in with the other volatile, aggressive emotions, McCord thought. He should be able to detect some remnant of Pru's glowing pride in him. She had certainly made it plain enough to his relatives and Devin Blanchard. Perhaps, if he concentrated, he could also detect a trace of her fierce refusal to believe he had done anything all that terrible three years ago.

Of course, he reminded himself, *she didn't know the whole story of what had happened three years ago.* McCord stared musingly out over the darkened sea and wondered if her staunch defense of him would survive if she knew all the facts.

The door behind him opened at that moment, and McCord felt another kind of tension in the atmosphere. He didn't turn his head, but he could almost read her mind. She was nervous again tonight about the prospect of sleeping with him.

The knowledge angered him because he wasn't quite sure how to counter her high-strung emotions.

"I warned you it wouldn't be a pleasant visit. If you hadn't decided to ignore my plans to stay for only an hour or two, we could have been long gone by now." He felt compelled to point that out and then instantly wished he hadn't sounded so aggressive. He could feel her stop halfway across the room.

"Your mother would have been crushed."

"She would have survived. She's survived the past three years, hasn't she? Besides, she set us up, tried to force us to stay by telling us about her plans for the evening."

"She was desperate," Pru said gently.

"You know how I feel about being manipulated."

"I know." There was a pause and then Pru went on in a cool, polite tone, "Thank you for not making a scene and insisting we leave when I told her we'd stay. I appreciate the fact that you didn't override my decision."

He got up out of the chair in a swift, tense movement, his anger growing. When he swung around to confront her, he found her standing several feet away. Her pale yellow nightgown flowed around her, making her look like a ghost in the shadows. She watched him with wary eyes.

"I decided you might as well learn your lesson the hard way," McCord said roughly. "Maybe after tonight you won't be so eager to restore the bonds of family harmony. What did Carrie say to you out there on the deck?"

She lifted one hand and let it drop back to her side. Slowly she trailed over to the window. "She's afraid."

"Afraid Kyle will lose his position as head of Mc-Cord Enterprises if my parents and I resolve our little disagreement?" he scoffed.

"Something like that."

He felt a flash of amusement. "Even though you'd spent most of the evening assuring everyone I was a farmer at heart and wouldn't be happy running the corporation?"

"She doesn't believe me."

McCord shrugged. "Who would? If I were in charge of McCord Enterprises, I'd easily triple my income, not to mention getting my hands on a lot of fringe benefits and a big chunk of real Southern California power."

"You make plenty of money working for J.P.," she tossed back tightly. "And your power is the ability to make a desert bloom, not force a million-dollar real estate deal to go through."

"Haven't you learned that when it comes to money and power one never has enough?"

"That's nonsense."

"You think so? Go ask Carrie. Or my brother, or Devin Blanchard, or my parents." He was goading her, and he knew it, but he couldn't seem to help himself. It was as if he suddenly had to test her, even though he knew she wouldn't falter. Maybe it wasn't so much a matter of testing her as it was a question of reassuring himself.

"I don't care what the others think. I know you and I know you've got everything you need in your job with the Arlington Foundation."

He listened to the certainty in her voice and almost smiled. "Is that right?"

"Yes, it is, and you know it. Why are you behaving like this?" She glanced back over her shoulder, frowning at him.

He exhaled slowly. "Maybe because I've just had a lousy evening."

"It wasn't altogether lousy," she protested. "You and your father managed to talk politely at dinner."

"Only because you provided a neutral topic."

"The pros and cons of canal irrigation in sandy soil?" Pru's mouth tilted slightly. "Your father really got into that topic, didn't he? I think there is a lot of the farmer left in him, too, even if he did eventually found a corporation and make a fortune in business. Maybe it's a case of being able to take the man away from the farm, but not being able to take the farmer out of the man."

"My mother would shudder to hear you say that. She hated living on the farm. My brother didn't like it, either."

"But you were at home there." Pru nodded. "That's what I was trying to explain to everyone all evening."

"They didn't understand," McCord told her grimly, wondering if he did himself.

"They will. Someday." She turned back to stare out the window.

"Maybe. Maybe not." He came up close behind her and found her shoulders with his hands. Leaning down to nuzzle the curve of her throat, he felt the immediate tension that rippled through her. Instinctively his fingers tightened, and she tensed even more.

"McCord, I've been thinking." Her voice was husky and very faint.

"I know. You've been doing far too much thinking the past few weeks. I've got a better idea tonight." He urged her back against him until her soft, rounded derriere came into contact with the taut hardness of him. She could arouse him so easily, he thought in wonder. He doubted that she even realized the extent of her sensual power over him. Pru was sweetly naive about things like power.

"I'm serious, McCord." The words were a little breathless, but very intent. "I know we're married now—"

"Damn right, we're married." He slid his hands down to her hips, holding her tightly. Deliberately he moved his thighs against her in a slow, provocative motion. She shivered.

"But marriage wasn't something you really wanted, McCord. I know that. I realize you went through with it because of the baby and...and I appreciate it, but—"

"Show me," he growled.

"Show you what?" She sounded bewildered.

"How much you appreciate it."

She swallowed. "That's just it, McCord. I'm not sure that's a good enough reason to go to bed with you."

He froze, his fingers digging deeply into the soft curve of her thighs. "What are you trying to say, Pru?" He heard the ice in his own voice, but it was nothing compared to the chill in his gut.

"I'm just suggesting that until we work out the basics of this relationship of ours, perhaps it would be better if we didn't sleep together." She stood very still under his hands. "I know you don't love me and I—"

"They got to you, didn't they?" McCord interrupted savagely.

"Who?"

"Carrie and my parents and even Devin Blanchard. They managed to put a few doubts in your head, after all. Oh, you tried to play the loyal, supportive wife, and you did a hell of a job, but deep down you started asking yourself some questions, didn't you? It's occurred to you that a man wouldn't have become estranged from all of these nice, intelligent people if there weren't a fairly good reason. You're starting to wonder what really did happen three years ago."

She whipped around in his arms, her eyes huge in the shadows. "McCord, stop it! You know that's not true."

"Do I?"

"Yes, damn it, you do." She threw her arms around his neck and hugged him violently. "That's not the reason I was having second thoughts about . . . about our sleeping together."

"Are you sure?"

She looked up at him with pleading eyes. "I'm absolutely positive. You must believe me."

"You've never, ever refused to go to bed with me since you moved in with me," he pointed out coolly. "Nothing's changed in our relationship except that you've got a ring on your hand. Why should you refuse me now unless it's because you've had some second thoughts after meeting my family?"

She blinked and then her eyes narrowed unexpectedly. "Damn you, McCord, you're doing this deliberately, aren't you?"

"Doing what?"

"You're deliberately goading me into feeling I have to sleep with you in order to prove I believe in you."

"It's possible," he said carefully, "that I just need some reassurance."

The last of her shaky barriers collapsed completely under the admission, just as McCord had suspected they would. Pru muttered something slightly incoherent and leaned into him, her arms tightening around his neck.

"Talk about manipulation," she grumbled against his chest.

"Let's not talk about it," McCord whispered thickly as he slid his fingers under her hair and found the nape of her neck. "Let's just go to bed where we belong." He tipped her head up and brushed his mouth lingeringly over hers. When he felt her instant response, the last of his inner tension faded to be replaced by the full force of his need.

He untied the laces at the top of her nightgown and slipped the garment off over her head. The fabric fluttered unheeded to the floor as McCord examined his wife in the moonlight. He knew she didn't think of herself as small for a woman. After all, she was five and a half feet tall. But to him she seemed delicate and fragile and soft. He worried about her carrying the burden of his baby.

She smiled up at him as if she sensed what he was thinking. Then she reached out to take hold of his hand.

Her eyes never left his face as she conveyed his palm to her breast and held it there.

"Sweetheart," he muttered, feeling his body react powerfully as he felt the response of her nipple under his palm. "You don't know what you do to me."

"Show me," she challenged softly.

He didn't care that she was taunting him gently with his own words. All he could concentrate on in that moment was the need to have her touch him. He caught hold of her hand, just as she had taken his. Then he placed her fingers at the open V of his unsnapped jeans. McCord knew she felt the shudder that went through him.

"That's it, baby," he breathed urgently. "Touch me. It feels so good when you touch me like that."

She slid her hands inside the waistband of his jeans and pushed them down over his hips, taking his briefs along with the denim. Pru sank slowly to her knees in front of him as she worked the garments down his thighs to his ankles.

McCord thought he would come apart in a hundred tiny pieces when he felt the soft tendrils of her hair against his thighs. He hastily stepped out of the jeans, but Pru didn't get to her feet immediately. Instead he felt her palms slide around behind his legs as if she would hold him still. When he felt the light, excitingly damp touch of her mouth pressed intimately against him, McCord knew for certain he was going to shatter. His hands tightened fiercely in her hair, and he groaned beneath the sweet, worshipful caress.

"My turn," he whispered in a thick voice as he tugged her to her feet and led her over to the bed.

"McCord?"

"Hush. One good turn deserves another." He pushed her gently onto her back and knelt between her legs.

She cried out softly as he brushed the first kiss against the silk of her inner thigh. McCord was aware of a deep rush of pleasure as he heard and felt her uninhibited reaction. Then he moved closer to the heart of her passion, and very soon Pru was breathless and writhing beneath him.

When he finally moved up along the length of her to claim her body with his own, she reached for him with so much feminine urgency and need that McCord almost laughed aloud.

But the sound was trapped in his throat because his body was too taut with passion to allow the joyous, triumphant laugh to emerge. He held Pru instead, burying himself within her. She gasped and dug her nails into his back.

McCord waited for a moment, luxuriating in the warm, velvet dampness that gripped him so sweetly. When he could stand it no longer, he began to move, slowly easing himself almost completely out of her body.

Pru gave a tiny whimper of protest and lifted her hips to tempt him back into the depths.

"I'm not going anywhere, honey," McCord promised. He gently caught a nipple between his teeth and tugged. Then he drove slowly back into her, filling her thoroughly.

"McCord, you know how to drive me crazy."

"You're beautiful when you're crazy. I like making you go crazy. I like it very, very much."

He repeated the long, slow thrusts until he felt Pru tightening beneath him. The feminine strength in her at times like this always astonished and excited him. She clung to him as though she would never let go.

"Now, McCord. *Now.*"

He whispered something dark and hungry and surged into her one last time, feeling the tiny, shimmering waves of release grasp him and hold him. His own deep convulsion poured through him and into her. Together they rode the storm-tossed waves into the quiet pools that waited on the other side.

When it was all over, McCord rolled onto his back and wrapped an arm around Pru, cuddling her comfortably against his damp body. With his free hand he gently eased a heavy, twisting, tangle of hair out of her eyes.

"Sleepy?" he asked.

"Umm." Her eyes were closed.

He touched one rosy nipple. "Are your breasts going to start getting bigger?"

"I don't know. I'm a little vague on some of this yet. I've only had one visit with the clinic doctor, and I spent most of my time trying to absorb the shock of learning I was pregnant. There are a lot of questions I haven't asked." She yawned hugely.

"I'll go with you on the next visit," McCord decided. "We'll ask the questions together. I'm new at this, too."

"So I gathered." There was a smile in her voice.

"Pru?"

"Yes, McCord?"

"Was it a rough shock? Learning you were pregnant, I mean?"

"Let's just say I felt very disoriented," she said dryly.

"You should have told me at once."

Pru said nothing for a moment. "Good night, McCord."

"You're still feeling a little disoriented, aren't you?" For the life of him, he couldn't quite bring himself to let her drift off to sleep. "That's why you don't want to announce the pregnancy yet."

"I guess so."

"Or maybe it's because you're still in shock," he went on meditatively.

"Maybe." She didn't sound very interested. In fact, she sounded almost asleep.

McCord looked down at her. Pru's eyes were still closed, and her breathing was taking on the gentle pattern of sleep. He should let her get plenty of rest, he told himself. She was going to need strength during the next few months. He'd see to it that she took it easy and obeyed the doctor's orders. And he'd take the prenatal classes with her, too.

This was his wife and his baby. They were both an integral part of his life, and he wanted to make certain he was an integral part of theirs.

As he slipped into sleep, he could feel the satisfaction and possessiveness that flowed through him. It seemed to McCord that a lot of the tension that had been seeping out of the walls of the house and into the atmosphere had been dissipated by the act of making love to Pru.

MCCORD AND PRU WERE READY to leave right after breakfast the next morning. Pru was somewhat embarrassed by her husband's blatant desire to be gone from the home of his parents, but she knew she'd pressed her luck far enough. She didn't dare insist they stay any longer.

They did stay for breakfast, however. The entire family and Devin Blanchard sat around a broad glass table in the all-glass dining room and ate fresh strawberries and cheese omelets and coffee prepared by Sandra. Pru, who had suffered another irritating bout of morning sickness, didn't recover her appetite as quickly as she had the previous day.

Everyone except Carrie seemed willing to try to find innocuous topics of conversation. Carrie simply didn't say a word. Evelyn kept sneaking covert glances at her son until Pru wanted to reach out and assure her it wouldn't be another three years until she saw him.

Devin Blanchard was the most at ease in the group, and Pru found herself talking freely with him as the others strained for neutral, polite ground.

He took her aside shortly before she and McCord were due to leave. It was the first time Pru had been alone with Blanchard, and when she looked at him she thought she saw sympathy and understanding in his eyes.

"It looks like you may be able to do something for this family they haven't been able to do for themselves, in spite of all their money and clout," he said quietly.

"I don't know," she answered wistfully. "They're a very stubborn lot."

"Not surprising when you realize just how bad things were three years ago. You've heard about Laura Reynolds?"

"Yes."

"She was like a daughter to Hale and Evelyn. The daughter they never had. They loved her."

"I see."

"She was very beautiful, very loving."

"From the sound of things she must have been somewhat headstrong and perhaps unstable."

Devin frowned. "You're referring to the fact that she killed herself in that crash?"

"Anyone who does a hundred miles an hour on an L.A. freeway must know the risks she's taking."

"She was distraught that night."

"So I hear. A broken engagement isn't a good enough excuse for that kind of idiocy," Pru said hardily.

"Is that what McCord told you? That she was upset because he broke off the engagement?" Devin shook his head sadly. "I'm afraid there was a lot more to it than that. Maybe you should know the whole truth before you make any judgments, Pru."

Pru lifted her chin and said proudly, "If there's any more I need to know, McCord will tell me in his own good time."

Devin's mouth kicked upward in reluctant admiration. "I can see why he thinks he's found a treasure in you. Not many women would trust him so completely. Not after what happened between him and Laura Reynolds."

At that moment Pru spotted Evelyn in the hall and seized on the opportunity of getting away from Devin Blanchard. She didn't want to hear any family secrets from him, she decided.

"There you are, Evelyn," Pru called cheerfully, just as McCord passed his mother in the hall with the luggage. "I almost forgot. I wanted to be sure you and Hale and Kyle and Carrie and Devin had an invitation to J.P.'s first annual ball."

Evelyn's expression was one of astonishment. McCord, overhearing the comment, slammed a short, narrowed look at Pru.

Pru didn't wait for either of them to say anything. Blithely she explained. "J.P. calls it a shindig, not a ball, naturally. He can't see himself throwing anything as fancy as a gala charity dance. At any rate, I'm stuck with having to organize the whole thing, and McCord and I will be forced to attend. It should be interesting, if nothing else. Why don't you think about coming down to La Jolla for it? We've got extra bedrooms, two of them, so there's plenty of room to stay with us."

"When is it?" Evelyn asked, casting an anxious look at Hale who was staring stonily at his new daughter-in-law.

"Saturday after next." She gave Evelyn the date. "You'll get a kick out of J.P. He's quite a character."

"Pru, it's getting late," McCord said from the doorway.

"I'm coming." She impulsively kissed Evelyn on the cheek, waved to Hale and smiled at Kyle and Carrie. "See you soon," she promised them all. As she turned to follow McCord out the door, her gaze collided with that of Devin Blanchard. "Do try to come, Devin," she said as warmly as possible. "I can get all the tickets I want. After all, I'm the coordinator for the thing. I'm not sure there's room at the house but—"

"That's all right," he said quietly. "If I can make it down to La Jolla, I'll stay in a hotel."

"Well," Pru said brightly, "that takes care of everything, doesn't it? I'd better get into the car before McCord leaves without me."

She hurried down the steps, slipped into the Ferrari and turned to wave at the cluster of people in the doorway. "I think your mother's crying," she said to Mc-Cord as he put the car in gear.

"Does that surprise you?"

"No, I guess not." The beautiful home receded into the distance, and Pru sat back in her seat.

"Don't get your hopes up, Pru," McCord remarked. "I doubt if they'll show up."

"Want to bet?" Pru smiled to herself, feeling smugly hopeful.

FOUR DAYS LATER Pru looked up from her desk in the tiny editorial office of the Arlington Foundation headquarters and decided there was one overriding reason why she shouldn't have run away from Case McCord.

She was swamped with work trying to catch up. Nobody had bothered to take care of her job in her absence. Apparently everyone had been under the impression she was only temporarily gone.

"I told everyone you'd be back right quick," J.P. had explained cheerfully when she'd walked into the office the day after returning to La Jolla. "That McCord may be bullheaded at times, but he ain't completely stupid." Sitting behind his inlaid desk, which was decorated with silver fittings and a set of gilded bullhorns in front, J.P. had appeared quite satisfied with himself. He'd had his dark green lizard skin boots propped on the desk, and his mint-green Stetson hung on one of the horns in front.

McCord, who was in the hallway behind Pru overheard the remark and came to stand in the doorway. "Thanks for your faith in my mental abilities, J.P. What the hell has everyone been up to while I've been gone? The report on the Maraku irrigation project still isn't out of typing, and Harve says you didn't call the meeting to discuss the soil conservation program."

"Well, son, to tell you the truth, we all just sort of sat around and played with our toes while worrying ourselves sick wondering how long it would take you to grovel your way back into Miss Pru's affections. But I guess we can all relax now that you've put a ring on her finger, huh? 'Bout time."

Pru stepped between the two men before McCord could make his retort. "How are the plans for the ball going? Did Mary Ann talk to the caterers?"

"Yeah, but I think there was some problem about the menu. Seems like the caterer didn't want to use my recipe for chili, and he became downright belligerent when she told him I wanted jalapeño-flavored corn bread."

"No kidding? Perhaps that's because your chili recipe is hot enough to set fire to any drapery and furnishings that happen to be nearby. And whoever heard of jalapeño-flavored corn bread?"

"I'll bet you've heard of it," J.P. said slyly.

"Only because I had the poor taste to be born in Spot, Texas." Pru stifled a groan. "I guess I'd better talk to Mary Ann first thing."

After that, she'd been immersed in work. But it was good to be back, she decided as she got her head above the stack of papers on her desk four days later. Her welcome from Martha and Steve had certainly been genuine and heartfelt. She'd had to hide a smile while she'd listened to Martha's complaints about McCord's foul temper during the week he'd spent trying to track her down. Steve's relief upon Pru's arrival was so visible she could only assume his life had been fairly miserable after the big departure scene, too.

There had been no word yet from Evelyn or any of the other McCords, so Pru was still keeping her fingers crossed that they would show up for the ball a week from Saturday. Every little step toward one another would help, she assured herself as she finished editing an article on insect problems in a tiny South American country. The man who had done the initial research was brilliant when it came to insects. Unfortunately he had never learned to spell.

The knock on her office door brought Pru's head up in frowning surprise. When she had her door closed, it was understood she was in the midst of editing and didn't want to be disturbed. Even J.P. respected the closed door.

"Come in," she said formally.

She was startled to see Carrie McCord walk into the small office. Her sister-in-law moved more awkwardly than ever beneath the weight of her advanced pregnancy, and there was no warmth in her eyes as she came to stand in front of Pru's desk.

"Hello," Carrie said evenly. "I've come to talk business with you, Mrs. Prudence McCord." The sarcasm on the Mrs. made Pru wince.

"What kind of business?" Pru asked warily. Her sister-in-law put a hand behind her back to rub her spine. It was obvious she was physically uncomfortable today. "Why don't you sit down?"

"I think," Carrie said deliberately, "that we should go someplace private."

"Why, Carrie?"

"Because I want to find out how much this is going to cost us, and I hate to discuss money in public, don't you?"

Pru held her breath. "How much what is going to cost you?"

"Buying you off, naturally. What did you think I meant? Kyle and I are prepared to make it worth your while to file for divorce immediately."

8

"WHERE ARE WE GOING?" Carrie demanded as Pru bustled her out to the foundation parking lot and into her small compact. "I want to talk to you alone."

"Don't worry, we'll be alone at the house at this time of day. The housekeeper will have left for the day by now, and the gardener has probably gone surfing," Pru said grimly. She climbed into the driver's seat and turned the key in the ignition.

"What about Case?"

"What about him? Don't you want him to hear this fabulous offer you're going to make to me?" Pru swung the little car out onto the palm-lined street. She was aware of her sister-in-law twisting uncomfortably in the seat beside her. In spite of the anger pulsing through her, Pru felt obliged to ask, "Are you all right, Carrie?"

"I'm fine," Carrie muttered. She stopped massaging her lower back and reclined wearily. "I didn't come here to see Case. I came to see you."

Pru sighed. "Don't worry. We're not likely to run into him at the house. He's got a series of research staff meetings today that will probably last until five or six o'clock."

There was silence in the small car until Pru pulled into the McCord drive. In spite of her tense, bitter mood, Carrie couldn't quite hide her surprise when she saw the lovely home.

"I didn't realize Case had done this well for himself," Carrie said hesitantly as she got out of the car and followed Pru into the house. "He left just about everything behind when he and his father quarreled. And I know Hale has never given him a dime."

"What did you think McCord had been doing for the past three years? Working in a fast-food restaurant to make ends meet? He's a very intelligent man, and what's more, he's a survivor. He's the kind who always lands on his feet. As my Aunt Wilhelmina would probably say, 'put him down in the middle of a cow pasture and he'd make a fortune selling manure.' Come on, Carrie we'll go out into the garden. It's cool out there. I'd offer you some lemonade, but under the circumstances I'm not feeling terribly sociable."

Carrie followed Pru through the wide, airy hall and out into the lush gardens at the back of the house. Pru noted that her sister-in-law was still having trouble assimilating the fact that McCord hadn't exactly been living in poverty since he'd been estranged from his family. She also noticed, in spite of herself, that Carrie still seemed to be in some physical discomfort.

Pru thought about her own pregnancy. She wanted to ask Carrie what it really felt like to be almost nine months along, but she didn't bother. They were hardly sisters.

"I think I should warn you," Pru said almost gently as she and Carrie sat down in white wicker chairs, "that if you make me an offer, you'll only make a fool of yourself. It would be better for future family relations if you just decided to turn this little session into an impromptu visit."

Carrie's chin came up aggressively. "You think you've done very well for yourself, don't you? You've come a long way from that dull little town in Texas, haven't you? You've even lost your accent. Good manners and enough money for good clothes can really camouflage a lot, can't they?"

Pru was jolted by the unexpected nature of the attack. "What did you do, Carrie? Hire a private detective to check out my background?"

Carrie tried to look casual about the matter, but there was a dark red flush on her cheeks. "It didn't take him long. Just a couple of days to verify that you were born to some cheap little truck-stop waitress who slept with just about every trucker who came along. None of them stayed around long enough to marry her, though, did they? You don't even know who your father was."

Pru came out of the chair, shaking with a rage that was unlike anything she had ever known before. "Shut up, Carrie! Do you hear me? Just shut up before I lose what's left of my temper. *And leave my mother out of this.* You can insult me all you like, but if you open your mouth about her one more time, I won't be responsible for my actions. The only reason I'm keeping my hands off you right now is because you're nine months' pregnant."

Carrie flinched, but she didn't back away from the firefight that had erupted. "You must have thought you'd landed on easy street when you became Case McCord's mistress. He must have looked pretty good to you after what you'd seen in Spot, Texas. You should have been content with that. How did you ever talk him into marriage? After all, you lived openly as his mistress for three months, I'm told. If he was getting what he wanted from you, why should he bother with marriage? Case isn't the noble type, believe me. Laura Reynolds found that out the hard way. You must be something else in bed. But once you realized just how big the prize really was, I'll bet you didn't rest until you'd somehow talked Case into putting a ring on your finger. What did you do? Get him drunk one night and drag him over the border into Mexico for a quickie wedding?"

"Carrie, I'm warning you, don't say anything more. You don't know what you're doing."

"Oh, yes, I do. You'd better remember that it's almost as easy to get a divorce these days as it is to get married in the first place. When McCord gets tired of playing house with you, you'll find yourself out on the street."

"That's my problem." Pru was trembling with the force of her fury. "If you're so sure that's what's going to happen, why are you here this afternoon?"

"Because I don't want to see Evelyn and Hale dragged through an emotional wringer because of a mercenary little bitch who thinks she can make life even easier for herself by patching up things between Case and his family."

"I don't think you give a damn about Evelyn and Hale," Pru said bluntly. "The only thing you care about is protecting your husband's position in McCord Enterprises."

"Kyle's worked long and hard at building the corporation into something more than even Hale imagined it could be," Carrie snapped. "I won't stand aside and see everything my husband's done go down the drain. McCord Enterprises is my child's future. You're not going to steal it."

"I've told you and everyone else that McCord would never be happy running McCord Enterprises!"

"But will you be happy until he reclaims what he probably feels is his heritage? I doubt it. Anyone who's come as far as you have from Texas dirt isn't going to stop now. Not unless she gets a better offer."

"Which you're prepared to make, I suppose?" Pru demanded sarcastically.

"Yes." Carrie challenged her with painfully bright eyes.

"How can you possibly offer me enough to make me walk away from all the McCord family money?" Pru taunted furiously.

Carrie drew herself up stiffly and then winced. Her hand went to her stomach. She caught her breath and continued. "I'm prepared to offer you a large lump sum to leave Case McCord. It won't be anything close to what you think you might be able to drain out of the McCords over the next few years, but it is a great deal of money. And it's *guaranteed* money. You could easily wind up with nothing if you try to play games with the McCords."

"Why should I accept?"

"Because," Carrie said, putting down her ace with grim relish, "if you don't, I will see to it that Case and his parents all see the report I got back from the private investigator."

Pru closed her eyes briefly and shook her head in pity. She turned away and took a few steps toward the flower bed. When she opened her eyes, she was staring at the picture-perfect roses Steve had been nursing under

McCord's guidance all spring. "Oh, Carrie, you're way off base. You don't know what you're doing."

"Don't try to bluff me, Pru. You can't possibly want your husband to know about your past. And even if you thought he could accept it, do you think Hale and Evelyn will? How do you think they'll react to the news that their new daughter-in-law is the illegitimate daughter of a Texas truck-stop waitress?"

"McCord already knows all there is to know about me," Pru said simply. "And I really don't care if Hale and Evelyn find out. I'm sorry to pull the teeth out of your little blackmail scheme, but the truth is, you can't threaten me that way."

"I don't believe you!" Carrie put her hands on the arms of the chair and heaved herself out of it. She was almost shouting now.

"It's the truth." Pru turned back with a slight smile. "If you want to verify it, stay for dinner this evening and bring the subject up with McCord. I'd advise you to do it tactfully, however. My husband is very protective of me. He won't take kindly to any insults."

Carrie stared at her with widening eyes. "I can't believe he married you. I can't believe it. He turned his back on Laura who loved him so much. Laura, who came from a good family and who was so beautiful. She was like a daughter to Evelyn, and McCord knew it. Everyone loved her."

"Except McCord, apparently. Carrie, you can't force love. There must have been good reasons why McCord broke off the engagement. He probably knew he and Laura wouldn't be happy together and saw no reason to put them both through a farce of a marriage. He was not responsible for her wild behavior after that."

Carrie took a step forward and stumbled slightly. Her lovely face grew momentarily taut with pain. "You don't know, do you? You really don't know what happened three years ago."

Pru saw the way Carrie was clutching at her lower back. "Carrie? Are you all right?"

"I told you, I'm fine," Carrie snapped. Then she gave a soft, muffled cry and grabbed at the arm of the chair. "Oh, my God," she whispered.

Pru leaped for her, catching Carrie before she fell and easing her down into the chair. "It's the baby, isn't it?"

"It can't be. I'm not due for another couple of weeks." She gasped again, and a flash of anxiety went through her eyes as she looked helplessly up at Pru. All Carrie's anger and dislike vanished to be replaced by the unsettling fears of incipient motherhood. "They say the first one is always late. This can't be happening. Not here. Not now. What am I going to do?"

"As it happens," Pru announced with determined cheerfulness, "I've been reading some books on the subject lately. Luckily for you, I'm a fast reader. Can you make it to the car?"

"Yes, I think so. I've still got some time. At least, I think I do. Oh, Lord, I didn't know it would happen like this. I wanted Kyle with me. I don't want to be all alone."

"I'll call him as soon as we get you to the hospital." Pru was gently guiding Carrie out of the garden.

"It'll take him hours to get here, even if you locate him right away. I'm going to be all alone." There were tears in Carrie's eyes.

"No, you are not going to be all alone," Pru said stoutly as she eased Carrie into the back seat of the compact. "You've got mé. Like it or not, we're sisters-in-law, remember? I'm family and I'm here. You won't be alone."

Whatever Carrie intended to say to that was lost beneath another wave of pain. By the time she recovered, Pru already had the car out of the drive.

Carrie's contractions were coming more frequently by the time Pru reached the hospital. The Emergency Room staff wasted no time. Pru stayed close to the bed as Carrie was whisked down the hall and into an elevator. When she offered her hand to Carrie, Pru was amazed by the desperate strength with which her sister-in-law grabbed it.

"Aren't we supposed to be counting or something?" Pru asked gently.

Carrie groaned. Her nails dug into Pru's palm. "I'm scared," she whispered.

A labor room nurse leaned over Carrie to undress her. "No need to be scared. It's going to be mighty uncomfortable for a while and a whole lot of hard work, but there's nothing to be afraid of. You're going to be just fine." She flashed a quick glance at Pru. "You're a member of the family?"

"Yes," Pru said calmly.

Carrie opened her eyes for a moment and essayed a weak smile. "She's my sister-in-law."

"Good," said the nurse. "She can stay with you until your husband gets here."

Pru smiled down at Carrie. "If you'll let go of my hand for five minutes, I'll go call him."

Carrie winced and reluctantly released Pru's fingers. "I'm sorry," she said.

"No problem. I'll be right back."

Carrie's head moved in a restless negative motion on the pillow. "No, Pru. I meant I'm sorry about...about everything. I behaved like a fool. I want you to know that Kyle doesn't even know I'm here. This fiasco was all my idea."

"Forget it," Pru advised. She patted Carrie's hand reassuringly.

"Kyle won't be able to get here in time," Carrie fretted.

"I keep telling you, you won't be alone." Pru went to find a phone.

KYLE MCCORD ARRIVED SHORTLY after his brand-new baby son. He found his wife asleep and his new sister-in-law sitting beside the bed, reading a magazine. When he came through the door, his gaze went first to the exhausted face of his wife and then to Pru, who smiled at all the anxious questions she saw in his eyes.

"Everything's fine, Kyle. Congratulations. You've got a beautiful baby son."

"Carrie's okay?"

"Just tired," Pru assured him, getting up out of the chair. "Here, why don't you sit down? I'm sure she'll be happy to see you when she wakes up."

"You're the one who took care of her? Got her to the hospital?" Kyle gave Pru a measuring glance that she decided must be a typical McCord family trait.

"I was the only one around at the time," Pru said dryly.

"You didn't have to stay with her."

"She's family," Pru murmured.

Kyle's gaze narrowed slightly and then he glanced again at his sleeping wife. "She must have come down here to see you."

"Yes."

"She was very upset about my brother's marriage." Kyle sounded as though he were feeling his way through a minefield.

"I know."

Kyle drew a breath and said bluntly, "I'm sorry if she said or did anything to insult you. She's been very emotional during these last few weeks."

"Perfectly understandable," Pru replied lightly. "Stop worrying about it, Kyle. Everything is just fine."

"Are you sure?"

"I'm sure."

He paused. "Does Case know?"

"I called him shortly after the baby arrived. He should be here soon."

Even as she spoke, the door opened to reveal McCord. "He's here now," he said softly. "Congratulations, brother, I understand you have a son."

Kyle nodded, the pride of fatherhood lighting his eyes. "That's what they tell me. I was supposed to be around for the big event, but Pru and Carrie had to handle everything all by themselves."

McCord grinned faintly. "Definitely women's work."

Kyle seemed surprised by his brother's easy smile. Slowly he responded, relaxing at last. "I agree. If you want to know the truth, I'm kind of glad I missed the delivery room drama. You know how squeamish I am."

"Both of you had better hush up," Pru advised in a low, scolding tone. "You'll wake, Carrie."

Carrie stirred beneath the sheet and sleepily opened her eyes. "I'm awake. Is that you, Kyle? It's about time you got here."

Kyle went over to the bed and took his wife's hand. "If you'd been at home where you're supposed to be, I would have been around to do my part of this. Just think, I went to all those classes and read all those books for nothing. What the hell did you think you were doing driving down here all by yourself?"

"I thought I had another couple of weeks before I had to worry." Her eyes met Pru's. "I just wanted to talk to Pru."

It was McCord who asked the next question. His voice was a little too quiet. "What did you want to talk to her about, Carrie?"

Carrie bit her lip. "Please," she whispered, "I'm very tired."

"She certainly is," Pru announced. "Let's go get a cup of coffee, McCord. We can come back later." She took a firm hold on his wrist and led him from the room.

"All right, Pru," McCord said bluntly as they walked into the cafeteria. "Tell me what this was all about. Why was Carrie here today?"

Pru set her coffee cup on the tray beside his. "She came to see me."

"What about?"

"Don't look so suspicious, McCord. She just wanted to get to know me better, that's all. A sisterly visit."

"Sure. And if I buy that one, you've got a nice bridge you can sell me, right? Come off it, Pru. Tell me what happened."

Pru sat down across from him and folded her arms on the table. She smiled enigmatically. "Carrie achieved her purpose, that's all."

"In what way?"

"She got to know me a little better."

McCord eyed her with a hooded gaze. He said nothing for a moment while his agile brain turned over the various possibilities. "She tried to buy you off, didn't she?"

Pru blinked in astonishment at his accurate guess. Her reaction gave away the truth. "Now, McCord."

He slouched back in the booth, his mouth twisting wryly. "What a little idiot."

"Me or Carrie?"

"Carrie. She should have known it would be a wasted trip."

Pru was warmed by the implicit faith McCord was showing in her. "She didn't know me very well. She knows me better now."

"Told her to go to hell, huh?"

"I told her she'd made a mistake."

McCord grinned and reached for his coffee. "A big one. There are only a small number of reasons you'd walk out on a man, Pru. Money isn't one of them."

"You sound very sure of yourself."

"I am," he said simply. "Unlike my sister-in-law, I've had several months in which to get to know you."

WHEN PRU AND MCCORD walked back into Carrie's room sometime later, they found the new parents inspecting the son they had produced. The baby had been brought into the room to nurse and was now sleeping contentedly in Carrie's arms. Pru joined in the general admiration, privately wondering if her baby would have the same wisps of dark hair.

"He's beautiful," she murmured.

"Why do women always say that about babies?" McCord complained good-naturedly as he studied the tiny scrap of humanity.

"Because it's a fact," Pru declared staunchly. "Isn't that right, Carrie?"

Carrie glanced uneasily at McCord before nodding. "When you work this hard to create one, you're bound to think it's beautiful. It's only natural for women to be emotional about babies. Men don't always understand how a woman feels when she's pregnant."

There was an awkward silence in the room that Pru didn't understand. She saw the suddenly shuttered look in her husband's eyes and didn't understand it, either. Kyle rushed to cover the small pause. "We called Mom and Dad a few minutes ago. They're thrilled."

"They should be," McCord said calmly. "The dynasty is now assured."

Kyle looked at him. "What's that supposed to mean?"

McCord shrugged. "Isn't it obvious? Now there's someone in line to step into your shoes when you're ready to hand over the reins of McCord Enterprises."

Kyle wrapped one hand around the railing of his wife's bed. His expression was cool, but that didn't hide the intensity in his eyes. "Meaning you're really not interested in taking back your old job?"

"I wouldn't be interested in a million years, Kyle. Weren't you listening at all to what Pru said the other night? I'm a farmer at heart."

Carrie stiffened. The baby in her arms whimpered in his sleep, and his mother instantly relaxed her grasp on the infant. "But if things were patched up between you and Hale..."

McCord glanced at Pru, his eyes brilliant. "Even if my wife pulls off that trick, it wouldn't make any difference as far as my future is concerned. I've got everything I want."

"You're telling the truth," Carrie said in mingled surprise and relief. "Aren't you?"

Pru was shocked. "Of course he's telling the truth. McCord always does. He's much too stubborn and proud to lie. You should know that. Come on McCord, let's go home. I'm getting hungry, and Carrie would probably like some rest. We'll stop back to visit tomorrow." She took McCord's hand and started to lead him from the room. At the doorway she had a last-minute thought. "You'll stay with us tonight, won't you, Kyle?"

"To tell you the truth, I hadn't given much thought to where I'm staying. Are you sure you have room?"

Carrie laughed softly. "Don't worry about it, Kyle. I saw your brother's home earlier today. There's plenty of room. Believe me, they're not living in some run-down little studio apartment. I think you're in for a surprise."

Kyle raised his eyebrows. "I doubt it. You forget I've known Case since I was born. My brother would survive very nicely in whatever situation he found himself."

Carrie smiled across the room at Pru. "That's funny," she said. "Pru said very much the same thing, although she phrased it a little less elegantly. Something about being able to drop Case into a cow pasture and watch him make a fortune selling manure."

"Is that right?" McCord gave Pru a shrewd smile. His eyes were gleaming. "I'm not sure where Pru gets all this boundless faith in me."

"Never mind," Pru said, vaguely flustered. "It's time to go." She urged him through the door, aware that Kyle was smiling behind her.

"A fortune in manure?" McCord repeated with grave interest as he walked down the hospital corridor beside his wife.

"It's an old Aunt Wilhelmina saying."

"Ah. Have you ever noticed how your Aunt Wilhelmina's sayings bear a striking similarity to some of J.P.'s?"

"It's crossed my mind from time to time," Pru admitted.

"Someday," McCord said thoughtfully, "we'll have to introduce them to each other."

Pru grinned. "That's a thought."

KYLE SHOWED UP on his brother's doorstep around eight-thirty that evening. He looked weary but happy.

"Mom and Dad are sure going to get a kick out of the kid," he told McCord and Pru as they sat talking in the living room. "They've been wanting a grandchild ever since you and Laura—" Kyle broke off abruptly, turning red in the face. "Sorry," he muttered. "That was stupid of me."

"I won't argue with that." McCord got to his feet and reached for the brandy bottle. "Here, have another drop of the good stuff. You've had a big day."

Kyle massaged his temples, leaning back in his chair. "That's for sure. I nearly went out of my mind when Pru phoned to tell me Carrie had gone into labor and that she was down here instead of at home. You want to watch out for pregnant ladies, Case. They do crazy things."

"I'll keep it in mind," McCord said neutrally.

Kyle looked at Pru. "I think the folks are going to come down here for that Arlington Foundation ball you mentioned."

"Really?" Pru was pleased.

"Mom's been working on Dad steadily since you left. Don't be surprised if they show up."

"We'll be ready."

"I guess Carrie and I will have to give it a miss now. Looks like we'll be learning how to baby-sit. Sorry. We would have liked to have come."

"Next year," Pru said reassuringly.

Kyle looked at his brother. "I get the feeling your new wife is going to single-handedly change a lot of things in the McCord family, big brother."

"If anyone can do it, she can," McCord replied easily.

Pru stirred on the couch. "I can't believe a bunch of intelligent people have acted this dumb this long. As my Aunt Wilhelmina would say, 'Stupidity is its own reward.'"

Kyle slanted her an odd look. "Your aunt may have had a valid point. In any event, I appreciate what you did for Carrie today, Pru. I can guess what she was doing down here in La Jolla. The very fact that she'd take off like that without letting me know where she was going is all the evidence I need."

"It doesn't matter anymore, Kyle," Pru said gently. When McCord sat back down beside her, she slipped her fingers through his. He gripped them tightly. "She was upset. I understood."

Kyle nodded. "Thanks. You're a very generous woman." He got to his feet and stretched. "Would you two mind if I hit the sack? I know it was Carrie who did all the work today, but I seem to be exhausted."

"Good night, Kyle." McCord nodded at his brother.

Kyle nodded once in return and left the room.

Pru turned to McCord, her eyes gleaming. "I told you they'd show up at J.P.'s ball."

"My parents?" McCord smiled. "So you did." He ruffled her hair with an affectionate gesture. "You're quite proud of yourself, aren't you?"

"I think it's downright silly for this family to have been at war for nearly three years for no real reason."

"My family is convinced it has a reason, Pru," McCord warned softly.

"Well, they don't. One of these days they'll admit it."

McCord sighed and poured himself another shot of brandy. "What did Carrie use to blackmail you with this afternoon?"

Pru cleared her throat, not deceived by the seeming casualness of the question. "McCord, it's over. I'd rather not talk about it. Carrie was upset and scared. She said some wild things that she now regrets. Let's let it drop."

"We will as soon as I know what lever she was using."

"McCord, there's no need to go into detail."

"That bad?" He cocked one brow in polite inquiry.

"Don't be an idiot," Pru snapped, incensed. "She just threatened to tell you and your parents about my past. She'd found out about Spot, Texas, and my mother and about my lack of a father and about how far I've come from Texas. Poor Carrie had some silly notion it would matter to you. I told you she wasn't thinking clearly." Then Pru groaned. "Now see what you've done? I wasn't going to tell you. How do you do it so easily, McCord?"

He grinned. "It's not me, it's you. You're lousy at keeping secrets. The only one you've ever managed to keep for any length of time was the one about being pregnant. Even there you got tripped up by outside forces."

"The letter from the clinic?" Pru shook her head. "It's strange to think my whole life was changed because of that bill."

"It didn't change your whole life. It just speeded things up a bit," McCord said. His eyes were suddenly very intent.

"What do you mean?"

"I would have come after you even if I'd never seen that bill, Pru."

She looked away from his glittering gaze. Her fingers twisted in her lap. "You would have?"

"Yes."

She smiled tremulously as she remembered what she had said earlier to Carrie. Case McCord was too proud and too stubborn to bother with lies. "I'm glad."

"Don't kid yourself," McCord growled as he pulled her into his arms. "I didn't have a choice. I wanted you back, Pru."

"I wanted you, too, McCord." She lifted her face for his kiss.

It wasn't until much later that night when Pru lay sleeping beside him that McCord realized she still hadn't admitted she loved him.

Her quiet stubbornness on the subject was beginning to bother him.

9

"You're IN LOVE with my son, aren't you?" Hale McCord asked without any warning as Pru paused midway through the vegetable garden to show off the peas.

Pru was so astonished by the unexpectedly personal question that she almost stumbled over a row of carrots. Then she wondered why she was hesitating to admit the truth aloud. Everyone seemed to know, including her husband. "Yes," she said calmly, as if it were the most natural thing in the world, "I am. Do you want to give me a hand with the carrots and the peas, Hale? Martha sent me out for spinach, but I think it's a little early for it yet."

"I haven't picked fresh vegetables in a while, but I haven't quite forgotten how." Hale smiled and leaned over to pull carrots from the ground with an easy, practiced movement.

Evelyn and Hale McCord had arrived an hour ago. Pru had been delighted to see them. They had been accompanied by Devin Blanchard, who was staying at a nearby hotel. Blanchard had politely declined the offer of a bedroom.

On the surface, McCord had been indulgent about the event, as if it really didn't matter to him one way or another what his parents did, but Pru was certain she'd seen initial surprise and then wary acceptance of the situation in his shuttered gaze.

Evelyn had clearly been slightly taken aback and then delighted by the obvious evidence of the level of success her son had reached in three short years. Hale had appeared curiously satisfied. He had said nothing about the fine home and the superb view, however, apparently content to let his wife exclaim over it.

When Evelyn had declared her intention to take a nap in order to get some rest before facing the big evening ahead, Pru had invited Hale out into the garden. McCord had disappeared into his study. Pru had been explaining the challenge of organic gardening to Hale when her father-in-law had interrupted to ask his blunt question.

There was silence for a moment after the interchange between Pru and Hale. They picked carrots and peas quietly together until Hale spoke again.

"Case seems to have done all right for himself."

Pru smiled slightly. "He's your son. Did you seriously imagine he hadn't been doing all right?"

"No. I hadn't lost complete track of him. I knew he was doing a fair amount of traveling and that he seemed to be establishing himself without any help from me or McCord Enterprises." Hale looked down at the small bundle of golden carrots he was holding. "But I certainly had no idea of just how high he'd climbed in the Arlington Foundation organization."

"J.P. depends on him. McCord plays a key role at the foundation."

"And I get the feeling you play a key role in Case's life." Hale gave her a shrewd glance. "After what he went through three years ago with his family, my son undoubtedly values unquestioning loyalty from those who claim to love him."

Pru's chin came up proudly. "I'm not a blind fool about loyalty, Hale. If there was a reason to question my husband's actions, I'd confront him and demand explanations. But so far I've had absolutely no reason to question him. I trust him completely. I can't believe he was any less trustworthy three years ago."

Hale stripped pea pods from a vine. "Perhaps he was a different man three years ago. Perhaps he's changed."

"Everyone changes, but I don't believe he had a drastically different sense of honor three years ago. His private code of ethics is too thoroughly ingrained in him. He was thirty-three years old then. An adult male and fully responsible for his own actions. I'm certain that, whatever happened, he was functioning within his own personal code. If he were to confront today the same situation he confronted three years ago, I have a hunch he'd handle it in very much the same way. Be honest, Hale. I'll bet your son grew up early, didn't he? He hasn't been a child for a long, long time."

"The thought doesn't appear to worry you. What would have happened if you had found yourself in the same position Laura Reynolds found herself in?"

Pru smiled. "I've always known where I stood with McCord. He's nothing if not honest. If Laura Reynolds was truly shocked by something McCord did or the way he acted three years ago, then frankly, she had only herself to blame. He wouldn't have pulled any rugs out from under her."

Hale shook his head in wry admiration of her staunch defense. "My son is a very lucky man. I hope he knows it."

Pru grinned. "Don't worry. I plan to remind him frequently."

Hale laughed aloud at that, the robust sound carrying easily through the open windows of the study. McCord, who had been standing at the window watching his wife and his father, found himself smiling slightly in response. He wondered what the joke was. It had been a long time since he'd heard his father's laugh.

Trust Pru to find a way to uncover it.

McCord's gaze went hungrily over the figure of his wife. She was wearing jeans, but she had a slouchy cotton knit top over them. He knew it was because she had reached the point where it was getting uncomfortable to fasten the top button of the denims. Last night in bed he had told her he was beginning to discover a new, added hint of roundness in her soft frame. Pru had told him it was his imagination, but McCord knew better. The changes taking place in her were both sexy and fascinating. They brought out all his protective instincts.

He had made love to her slowly and deliberately, drawing out the process until she was shivering and clinging to him. He had held off the final culmination, waiting expectantly for the words of love he'd been anticipating since the day of the wedding. But Pru hadn't spoken them.

McCord couldn't understand why she didn't admit what he could read so easily in her eyes. He knew she was in love with him. On the couple of occasions when he'd confronted her with the fact, she hadn't denied it. But although she was excitingly generous with her passion in bed, she had never yet whispered her love to him during their most intimate moments together.

McCord felt the instant changes that started taking place in his own body as thoughts of the previous night's lovemaking drifted through his head. With a small, muttered oath he turned away from the window. He had a long evening ahead of him before he could climb back into bed with Pru.

J. P. ARLINGTON HAD OUTDONE HIMSELF for the occasion of the first annual foundation shindig. He was wearing white. White hat, white shirt, white tie, white western-style jacket, white flared trousers and white leather boots. The outfit was accented with judiciously applied rhinestones and silver. The glittery touches circled the crown of the hat, sprinkled across the yoked shoulders of the jacket and formed long strips down the outside seams of the trousers. There was an additional wedge of silver on the pointed toes of the boots.

All in all, Pru decided in amusement, J.P. was quite a sight. Fortunately the guests loved the outrageous look of their host as well as some of the outrageous Southwestern food that sat side by side with elegant pâtés and choice canapés on the buffet table. J.P. was moving through the well-dressed crowd with ease, enjoying himself enormously.

The hotel ballroom the foundation had rented for the evening was lavishly decorated for the event. The white-and-gilt walls and ceiling sparkled beneath the light of two magnificent chandeliers. The dance floor was filled with couples enjoying the music of the excellent band playing at the far end of the huge room.

The opposite end of the room featured the large buffet where the chili and the jalapeño-flavored corn bread were moving quite well. When people commented on the unusual food choices, J.P. explained he liked to get back to his roots occasionally.

It was always interesting, Pru thought, how much easier it was to get large sums of money from people when they were surrounded by lavish hospitality. She had commented on that fact to McCord earlier in the evening when they had been dressing for the event.

"It seems wrong to have to put on such a lavish affair just to convince people to contribute to a foundation that's trying to do something about starvation," Pru had remarked.

"Honey, it's a cold, hard fact of life that it takes money to make money. Right or wrong, that's the way the world works," McCord had told her.

Pru had chosen a free-flowing yellow-and-green silk gown that fell lightly around her figure. She hadn't been able to get into the snug-fitting red gown she had originally planned to wear. While they were dressing, McCord had teased her gently about the small changes that were taking place in her figure, and she had made a face in the mirror.

To her surprise his expression had turned serious. He had come up behind her to help fasten a thin golden chain around her neck. "Are you going to hate being pregnant?" he'd asked.

"It's a little late to worry about that," she'd replied easily, reaching for her earrings.

He'd looked as though he'd wanted to say something else but hadn't been able to formulate the question. Instead he'd leaned down to kiss the nape of her neck, which had been left bare by her upswept hairstyle.

"You won't be alone when your time comes," he'd promised. "I swear I'll be there with you."

He'd been thinking about his sister-in-law's experience, Pru had realized. "Don't make any rash promises. J.P. is always sending you off to some exotic corner of the world. Heck, next week you get to go all the way to mysterious Nebraska to check out that corn experiment."

"What a thrill." He'd touched her cheek, meeting her eyes in the mirror. "I'm going to cut way back on the traveling, Pru. There are others who can handle that end of things. I'd rather spend my time in the experimental fields and the classroom. And with you and the baby."

"I'll hold you to that," Pru had said lightly.

Remembering the small scene in the bedroom, Pru took her eyes off J.P.'s vivid figure and scanned the room, looking for her husband. She finally spotted him introducing Devin Blanchard to an attractive young woman named Julia from the editorial staff. The social task over, McCord left Devin with his new acquaintance and moved off to join the group of men around J.P. Pru was thinking of how compelling her husband looked in his evening clothes when she heard her mother-in-law's voice at her elbow.

"This sort of thing is more work than fun for you and Case, isn't it?" Evelyn McCord asked as she and Hale moved up to stand beside Pru.

Pru laughed. "I'm afraid so. J.P.'s fortune forms the financial basis of the foundation, but outside contributions are vitally important. You'd be surprised how much money J.P. will pull out of the woodwork tonight. He'll ply everyone with his jalapeño martinis, and the first thing you know, money will be flowing in right and left. I've seen him at work before."

"What's Case's role in the money-raising efforts?" Hale asked with interest.

"Once J.P. gets going, he's pretty good at social chit-chat, but he relies on McCord to answer the technical questions a lot of potential contributors will ask."

"Unfortunately the net result is to leave you to fend for yourself most of the evening," Evelyn murmured.

"Oh, I don't mind. This is business, and I've got plenty to do. I'm the one who has to make sure we don't run out of food and that no one gets embarrassingly drunk or left forlorn in a corner. You know, the odd jobs."

Devin Blanchard's voice interrupted Pru before she could continue. He walked up to join the small group. "Does that mean you might be available to entertain one of your guests on the dance floor?"

Pru turned to smile at him. He had approached from the far side of the room. She wondered what had become of Julia. "I think I can sneak in a quick dance."

"Great." He nodded at Hale and Evelyn. "If you'll excuse us?"

"Of course," Evelyn said. "In fact, if I can talk Hale into it, we might join you on the floor. Haven't danced in ages, have we, Hale?"

"I doubt if I've improved since the last time," Hale warned good-naturedly.

The two couples slipped onto the crowded floor, and Pru soon lost track of her in-laws as Devin took her in his arms. She was surprised at the forcefulness of his hold. Automatically she tried to put a little distance between them.

"Sorry," Devin apologized at once. "Didn't mean to crush you. I just didn't want you bumping into that couple behind you." He smiled engagingly.

"That's all right," Pru assured him. "I'm so glad you could accompany Hale and Evelyn this evening."

"I think they wanted a little moral support. After three years of estrangement, they don't quite know how to deal with Case. Originally Carrie and Kyle were going to come with them, but those plans fell apart when their son arrived a couple of weeks early."

"I gather you're practically a member of the family in many ways."

"Practically," Devin emphasized quietly. "Not completely. There's a big difference, Pru, believe me."

Pru wondered at the faint trace of bitterness in his voice. "Does that bother you?"

He looked down into her questioning eyes. "I accept it. I'm paid very well and I can hardly complain."

"Then why does it bother you that you're not a McCord?" Pru asked before she could stop to think.

"Let's just say that not being a McCord puts some real limitations on an employee of McCord Enterprises."

"Such as?"

"It's basically a family business," Devin explained. "No matter how good I am or how much I'm trusted, I can only go so far in the organization. A McCord makes all the final decisions and the McCords split all the really big profits."

"Maybe that will change someday," Pru suggested.

"Not a chance. Not as long as there's a McCord male around."

Pru considered the situation. "If you feel that way about the matter, maybe you should go to work for another organization."

Devin favored her with a quick, rueful grin. "Are you kidding? Not many other corporations would match my present salary, and it would take years to work my way up to the kind of status I have now. The McCords listen to me and they trust me. It's the next best thing to actually being in charge. One of these days I may leave for greener pastures, but it would take a pretty good offer to lure me away."

He might resent the fact that he could never be president of the company, but he wasn't about to sacrifice his cushy position by going elsewhere, Pru realized. Devin Blanchard was an eminently practical man.

"It's obvious both Hale and Kyle value your abilities enormously," Pru said, striving for a diplomatic ending to the unexpected conversation.

Devin slanted her an amused glance. "Case valued them at one time, too. You'd never know it, but there was a time when Case and I were like brothers."

"Times change," Pru said cautiously.

"People change."

Pru remembered the conversation with her father-in-law in the garden. "Sometimes. I don't think McCord has changed all that much in the past three years, however. There's something very rock-solid about him. I'd be willing to bet he was always that way."

"You're really in love with him, aren't you?"

"It must be painfully obvious. You're the second person today to comment on it."

Devin looked down at her, concern in his eyes. "I recognize the signs because I saw them in Laura Reynolds."

"I'd rather not talk about her, Devin."

"Sure, I understand." He stopped dancing as the music came to a halt. He glanced over Pru's shoulder. "There go Hale and Evelyn out onto the terrace. Shall we join them? Your husband still seems to be occupied."

Pru glanced around. Everything appeared to be functioning smoothly. No one looked bored or uncomfortable, and the food supply was holding out well. There was no reason not to join the McCords on the terrace for a while. "Sounds good. It's hard to talk above the music, isn't it?"

"That's for sure." Devin led her through the open doors of the ballroom and out onto the lushly landscaped terrace.

"I don't see the McCords," Pru remarked.

"I thought I saw them come this way. Maybe they're over by the fountain." Devin started strolling casually toward the large stone fountain that dominated the hotel gardens. Pru fell into step beside him.

Back in the ballroom, McCord sensed a subtle change in the atmosphere. It was nothing he could name, but it was enough to make him turn his head and search for Pru. He caught sight of her just as Blanchard led her outside onto the terrace. McCord felt his gut tighten.

"Excuse me," he said to the middle-aged scientist with whom he had been discussing soil erosion, "I think I'd better check up on my wife."

The man nodded understandingly. "I'll catch you later. I want to hear about that trip you made to Africa. I've been very curious about what you actually saw."

"Later," McCord promised, and then he was striding through the crowded room.

He encountered his parents near a pair of open French doors. Hale and Evelyn were chatting with J.P. and apparently enjoying themselves.

"There you are, McCord," J.P. said loudly. "I was just explaining the secret of making a perfect jalapeño martini to your dad."

"Don't believe him," Hale said with a lazy grin. "J.P. was leaning on me pretty heavily for a contribution to the foundation. I recognize a pitch when I hear one."

J.P. chuckled, not bothering to deny it. "Your dad's tighter than bark on a tree."

"He just needs to be convinced," McCord said, looking at Hale. "My father likes hard evidence. He isn't easily swayed by sentiment."

Evelyn, at least, appeared to realize the underlying comment extended to more than just J.P.'s efforts to get a contribution from her husband. She stepped into the conversation before it could go any further in what she obviously had concluded was a dangerous direction. "Looking for Pru?"

McCord nodded abruptly. "I saw her go out onto the terrace."

"Hale and I could use some fresh air," Evelyn said quickly, "isn't that right, Hale? Why don't we go with Case?"

"I don't know about fresh air, but it might be a good idea to take a break from J.P. before he finds a way to part me from my money."

J.P. grinned broadly. "I'll be here when you get back."

McCord shrugged, not hesitating any longer. He didn't really care if his parents followed him. He just wanted to locate Pru and bring her back inside.

"This is certainly a lovely event," Evelyn remarked as she hurried to keep up with her son. "I must say the foundation does a first-class job when it comes to entertainment."

"It's a business expense. It'll pay for itself several times over in terms of contributions to the foundation." McCord quickened his pace when he realized he couldn't see Pru anywhere in the garden. There was a curious tension flowing in him now. He felt as if he were on the verge of combat. Telling himself that he was being ridiculous didn't do any good. Some primitive instinct had been aroused by the sight of Pru walking away with Devin Blanchard.

Then he heard her voice and started toward the fountain that was located on the other side of a tall hedge. Hale and Evelyn followed.

PRU CAME TO A FIRM HALT beside the fountain. "I don't see them, Devin. They must have gone in another direction. I'd better get back to the party before J.P. wonders what he's paying me for."

Devin shrugged. "I could have sworn I saw them come this way. Oh, well, no harm done. It feels good to get away from the crush for a while."

"If you'll excuse me," Pru began politely, only to stop when she felt Devin's hand clasp her wrist. She looked up at him with point-blank inquiry, and her voice hardened slightly. "What's the matter, Devin?"

"I brought you out here to talk to you, Pru."

"About what?"

"About your husband."

"I don't want to discuss him with you." She tried to pull her wrist free and was irritated when his hold tightened. "Please let me go."

"In a moment, I swear. Pru, this is for your own good."

"I doubt that."

"You have a right to know what really happened three years ago, and it's becoming damn obvious the McCords aren't going to tell you."

"You're wrong. My husband has already told me exactly what happened. I don't need to hear anyone else's version of the truth. Let me go, Devin. You're becoming annoying."

"Listen to me, Pru. I was there. I know the truth. And I know McCord hasn't told you what really went on. If he had, you wouldn't still be with him, believe me. You wouldn't trust him so completely."

She realized he was almost desperate to make his statement, and she wondered what drove him. "What makes you think my husband lied to me?" she demanded angrily. "McCord has never lied to me."

"I'm not saying he lied, only that he can't have told you the full truth. If he had, you wouldn't defend him so fiercely. In fact, if he'd told you what he did to Laura three years ago, you probably would never have married him!"

"That's the most asinine thing I've ever heard. One last time, Devin, let go of my wrist."

"Don't you understand?" Devin flared. "It wasn't just a broken engagement that tore Laura up so much that she killed herself on that freeway. There was a baby. Laura was two months' pregnant, and Case refused to marry her. Hale and Evelyn's first grandchild died along with the woman who was like a daughter to them. All because Case McCord wouldn't marry the woman he'd got pregnant. He told her to get rid of the baby if she wanted to continue the engagement. Laura nearly went crazy."

A woman's anguished gasp of dismay made Pru swing around in astonishment. She found herself confronted by McCord and his parents. Hale looked proud and grim. Evelyn was staring at Pru with such pain in her eyes that Pru almost cried, too.

Case McCord simply looked at his wife as if he were prepared for whatever verdict she chose to render. No one spoke.

Pru met her in-laws' unhappy expressions with a sense of utter amazement. "Is this the reason behind three years of stubbornness? You really believe McCord got Laura Reynolds pregnant and then threatened to break off the engagement if she didn't have an abortion?"

"Oh, Pru," Evelyn said miserably. "There was no need for you to know the whole truth. It's all in the past. I was so hoping it could stay there. It's caused so much pain and turmoil, and there's absolutely nothing anyone can do now to change it. We must all put it behind us and forget it. Three years is a long time. Everyone makes mistakes..." She turned a pitying gaze on her son. "But life goes on."

"For heaven's sake," Pru exploded. "I can't believe this."

"You have to believe it, Pru," Devin said flatly. "We do."

"I can't imagine why," she retorted.

Hale took a step forward as if to put a consoling hand on her shoulder. But he stopped when she glared at him. "I told you this afternoon that people change," he reminded her.

"And I told you that your son hasn't changed all that much in the past three years. He might be a little older and a little smarter in some ways, but fundamentally he's the same man now as he was then. I don't believe he would have acted any differently three years ago than he would act today if he were faced with a similar set of circumstances. If he refused to marry Laura, there was a damn good reason."

"He didn't want the baby," Evelyn whispered. "He told Laura he didn't want the baby."

"I suppose those were Laura's famous deathbed words?"

Hale and Evelyn looked at each other. "Well, yes," Evelyn admitted.

"Where is it written," Pru muttered, "that an angry woman is going to be inclined to tell the truth on her deathbed?"

"You don't understand, Pru. She *was* pregnant. The doctor confirmed it." Devin came up behind her and touched Pru's shoulder.

She stepped out from under his fingers. Her eyes swung to McCord, who was standing very still and utterly remote in the shadows. "What is this, McCord? You couldn't be bothered to defend yourself from Laura's accusations?"

McCord shrugged. "No one doubted Laura's side of things. She was an excellent actress. On her deathbed she gave a very heartrending performance, believe me."

Pru threw up her hands. "I can't believe I'm hearing this nonsense. Three years? Three whole years this family has been at odds because of Laura Reynolds's accusations?"

"They weren't false accusations," Devin said through gritted teeth. "Laura was pregnant, and he refused to marry her. He threw her out of his life when she refused to get rid of the baby. Ask Case, if you don't believe me."

"I don't have to ask him," Pru said, her voice tight with fury. "If Laura was pregnant and if McCord refused to fulfill his responsibilities, then there is only one explanation on God's green earth why he acted as he did."

"Why?" Evelyn McCord's single query was almost hushed.

"Because the baby wasn't his and McCord knew it!"

There was absolute silence from the small circle around Pru as they stared at her and tried to absorb the impact of her words.

"Furthermore," Pru continued aggressively, "the one thing McCord won't allow himself to be is manipulated. Any woman who tried to trick him into believing he was the father of her child so that she could force him to marry her was asking for trouble and should

have known it. What's the matter with you people?"
She turned on Hale and Evelyn. "McCord is your son.
You should have known him better than anyone. You
should have been able to figure out for yourselves that
there had to be more than Laura's side to the story."

"Is this what Case has told you?" Hale finally asked
tightly. His intent gaze went to his son.

"No, he didn't tell me the baby wasn't his. We never
discussed the matter. But there is no other explanation."

"How do you know that?" Devin snapped.

Pru put her hands on her hips. "Because I am the
world's leading authority on what Case McCord would
do if he got a woman pregnant. Why on earth do you
think he married me? We'd been living together openly
for nearly three months. He'd made it very clear he had
no interest in marriage. But when I accidentally got
pregnant and ran off, he came after me and demanded
I marry him. No ifs, ands or buts. No demands that I
have an abortion. No accusations of carelessness.
When the chips were down, McCord insisted on ful-
filling his responsibilities. He would have done the same
three years ago—if the baby had been his. Laura obviously had a lover and, as my Aunt Wilhelmina would
say, McCord clearly had no intention of picking up the
tab for some other man's stud services."

Pru didn't wait to see the reaction to her statement.
She whirled on her high heels and stalked over to
McCord. When she put a demanding hand on his arm
and looked up at him, she found his eyes gleaming with
dark fire.

"Take me back to the ballroom, McCord. You know
it isn't safe to leave J.P. alone in a roomful of potential

foundation contributors. He'll go crazy with the jalapeño martinis."

McCord took her arm in a grip of warm steel. "Right this way, honey."

They left the others standing by the fountain and walked silently back toward the brightly lit ballroom.

10

MCCORD HAD KNOWN the inquisition would come as soon as everyone walked into the house after the conclusion of J.P.'s fancy shindig. He had been expecting it ever since Pru had dropped her little bombshell. It was a rather touching tribute to her sweet streak of naiveté that Pru herself was startled by Hale McCord's demand for further explanations. There had been no opportunity earlier for his parents to corner McCord, probably because he hadn't felt like being cornered and had seen to it Hale and Evelyn were kept busy from the moment they reentered the ballroom. Devin Blanchard had disappeared. Apparently Pru had thought the matter settled.

McCord could have told her things weren't going to be that easy.

"I think," Hale said as he escorted his wife into the living room of his son's home, "that we deserve some further explanations."

McCord said nothing. Instead he headed for the brandy tray Martha had thoughtfully put out earlier. It was Pru who responded. She swung around to confront her in-laws.

"Further explanations about what?"

"You must realize what a shock this has been to us, dear," Evelyn said soothingly. "We had no idea about . . . about Laura having had a lover."

"Oh, that," Pru said, as if she really had put it all behind her. She frowned at McCord. "You did tell everyone at the time that the baby wasn't yours, didn't you, McCord?"

"I believe I did mention it." McCord poured his brandy, debated about pouring two more for his parents and finally decided it would be churlish not to offer them a drink. He tipped the bottle over two more glasses. "I also remember that no one was particularly interested in listening."

When he turned around to hand the brandy to his parents, he caught the full impact of their shocked gazes. Wordlessly they accepted the glasses. Hale downed half of his almost at once.

"Laura was dying," Evelyn whispered in a heartbroken voice. "She said she hadn't wanted to live after you rejected her and the baby."

"I know what she said." McCord went to stand near Pru, who was glowering at all of them. "I was at her bedside along with everyone else. There's nothing quite like the impact of a deathbed statement, is there?"

"We were all in shock," Evelyn said. Wearily she sat down, her eyes going to her husband's grim face. "She was so dear to us. We loved her like a daughter. And we were so certain the two of you were in love."

"Laura was in love with the idea of marrying into the McCord clan," McCord stated flatly. "She was not in love with me."

"She probably needed a sense of security after her father died," Evelyn suggested. "She felt alone in the world. We were the only family she had."

"Umm." McCord made no further comment. It had, after all, happened three years ago. There was no point resurrecting more than necessary.

"But if she was so determined to marry you," Hale pointed out with unerring logic, "why would she have taken another lover?"

"She didn't take *another* lover," McCord said. "She took a lover. It wasn't me. It was never me."

Pru's head snapped up as she realized the significance of his words. "You never touched her?" she asked in amazement.

"No." He was aware of what she was thinking. She knew his sensual appetites. From the moment he'd met Pru, he'd wanted to take her to bed. He'd made no secret of it. It was probably hard for her to imagine him involved in a chaste, platonic engagement. "She wouldn't let me put a hand on her, not even after we were engaged." McCord smiled wryly down at her. "I told you she was an excellent actress. She wanted all the McCords to believe she was the perfect, untouched angel who wouldn't think of soiling her wings by going to bed with a man without a ring on her finger."

Pru's cheeks turned a sudden, vivid pink, and her eyes slid away from his. McCord was instantly furious with himself as he realized she had misunderstood his meaning. The last thing he had wanted to imply was that he valued the kind of role Laura had played. He wanted to grab Pru and hold her until he'd explained he wanted nothing to do with a cold-hearted woman who used her body like a tool, withholding herself from a man until he had agreed to meet her terms.

But the damage was done, and McCord knew he couldn't correct it in front of his parents. He would only succeed in embarrassing Pru further.

"You never went to bed with Laura." Hale eyed his son speculatively. "And that's why you're so certain the baby wasn't yours. What happened the night she died, Case?"

McCord was irritated at the question. Right now he wanted to talk privately to Pru and instead he was having to rehash old history. With a muttered oath, he turned to face his parents.

"After a few months of playing the chaste ice maiden, Laura was suddenly very insistent on going to bed with me. Unfortunately for her, I had already decided I wanted out of the engagement. Her timing was bad, I'm afraid. When she failed in her seduction efforts, she panicked. She called me that night in tears and told me she had to see me. When I got to her apartment, she threw herself into my arms and told me she wanted to get married right away. The wedding date was still three months off, and I was naturally a little curious about the sudden rush. I was also a little suspicious. I had been for a while, if you want to know the truth. I told her I was seriously considering ending the engagement. That I wasn't sure we were right for each other and that I thought it would be best if we put everything on hold for a while."

"That's when she told you she couldn't wait? That she was pregnant?" Evelyn asked.

McCord nodded. "She gave me an ultimatum. Told me that I had to agree to marry her as soon as possible or she would tell the whole family she was pregnant with my child."

Out of the corner of his eyes, he saw Pru chewing on her lower lip. Now she knew where he got his dislike of ultimatums, McCord thought.

"You called her bluff?" Hale asked sharply.

McCord sighed and drained the last of the brandy. "I told her I had no intention of, uh, picking up the tab for someone else's stud services."

Pru winced and looked down at her folded hands.

"We argued some more, and eventually I left. The next time I saw her was in the hospital."

"Where she took what revenge she could get on her deathbed," Hale concluded. "You stated once that the baby wasn't yours and we all jumped down your throat. You never said another word on the subject."

There was silence in the room for a long moment. Then McCord spoke, feeling obliged to point out the obvious. "Nothing's changed. The situation is exactly the same as it was three years ago. You've still got my word against Laura's deathbed declaration. Why the big scene tonight?"

Hale looked at Pru. "Three years ago we saw you the way Laura wanted us to see you: a man with feet of clay. She was our dying daughter, and we were heartsick. But lately your wife has reminded us that we should know you well enough to realize you're not the kind of man who would shirk his responsibilities. We should have known that all along. Instead of seeing you through Laura's eyes, we're suddenly seeing you the way Pru does. The way we'd always seen you until that night three years ago."

"I think," Evelyn said quietly, "that once the shock had worn off, we wanted to believe you, but by then so much damage had been done. Everyone was so proud and stubborn. Neither side would give an inch. I can't believe we let these three years go by without trying to repair the breach. It took Pru to bring us to our senses."

"You believe me now because Pru believes me?" McCord asked. His mouth twisted sardonically.

Evelyn's expression was thoughtful, her eyes warm as they rested on her new daughter-in-law. "Let's just say that Pru has restored our perspective on the situation. She's reminded us of the kind of man you are. Seeing you again through her eyes has cleared away the fog of doubt and pain that Laura created. Poor Laura. If only we had realized what a troubled young woman she was."

Pru spoke up for the first time in several minutes. "You can't help someone who doesn't want to be helped. Laura made her own decisions, and no one is to blame for what happened three years ago."

Evelyn smiled. "Did my son really marry you because you're pregnant?"

Pru wrinkled her nose. "I'm afraid so. He was very insistent on marriage once he found out he was going to be a father. I hope you don't mind the prospect of being a grandmother for a second time?"

"I am absolutely delighted by the idea." Evelyn's face was alight with pleasure. She came across the room and hugged Pru. "I can't tell you how happy I am tonight, my dear. Thank you for everything."

Hale looked at his son. "You're a lucky man, Case."

"I know," McCord said. He put his arm firmly around Pru's waist. "If you'll excuse us, we're going to bed. It's nearly two in the morning, and Pru needs her rest these days." He steered her toward the hall while everyone murmured good-night.

Pru walked beside him without saying a word. McCord could feel the tension in her. It made him tense in reaction. When the door of the bedroom closed behind them, he turned her around to face him.

"I didn't want an untouchable angel who claimed she loved me and then had absolutely no problem resisting my lovemaking. I didn't want a woman who withheld herself from me as a means of manipulating me. I wanted a warm, generous, honest woman who, when she fell in love with me, couldn't resist me no matter how hard she tried. A woman who wanted me as much as I wanted her. A woman who believed in me completely. A woman I knew would always be loyal. A woman I could trust. I wanted you, Pru. Just the way you are."

"But you didn't want to have to marry me."

His hands tightened on her shoulders. "Sooner or later we would have been married, honey, believe me. It was inevitable. I've been getting too damn possessive where you're concerned. But when you gave me that ultimatum . . ."

"All you could think about was the last time a woman had given you an ultimatum," Pru concluded sadly. "I reminded you of Laura."

Irritated by her silly logic, McCord gave her a gentle shake. "No, you did not in any way remind me of Laura. But I'll admit I didn't like being threatened. I thought I could call your bluff and teach you a lesson in the process. I was certain you wouldn't have the nerve to actually leave me. But as my brother Kyle said, women sometimes do crazy things when they're pregnant."

"I suppose you and Kyle think you're authorities on the subject now?"

"We're fast learners." McCord pulled her close and kissed her firmly on the mouth. He could feel her standing stiff and tense in his hold. Deliberately he deepened the kiss, easing apart her lips until he could taste the warmth inside her mouth. When she whimpered softly and began to relax against him, he felt a surge of satisfaction and relief.

"How did you happen to find me with Devin at the fountain?" she murmured against his lips as she slipped her arms around his neck.

"I saw you leave the room with him." McCord nibbled her ear. "I went after you to bring you back. My parents just came along for the walk. We found you at the fountain just as you launched into your magnificent defense of my conduct three years ago. How the hell did you know Laura had been sleeping with someone else?"

"It was the only logical explanation. If you'd thought the baby was yours, you'd have done your duty."

"Thanks. I think." He nuzzled the nape of her neck, inhaling the sweet warm scent of her skin. "You're still convinced that's the only reason I married you, aren't you? Out of a sense of duty."

"You weren't rushing to marry me before you found out about the baby," she pointed out tartly.

Her obstinateness on the subject was really beginning to annoy him. McCord slid his hands down her back, easing the zipper of her gown. "You know there's a hell of a lot more than obligation involved. You know how much I want you, how much I like having you in my arms. *And you also know how much you like being in my bed.* Admit it, honey."

She shuddered delicately as the gown pooled at her feet. McCord reached out and turned off the light. In the shadows he could see Pru's eyes glowing with the soft light of her love. She smiled tremulously.

"I like being in your bed," she responded with amused obedience. "But, then, you already knew that."

He unfastened her lacy little bra and let the wispy garment flutter to the floor. "I know it, but I like hearing it."

"You're a greedy man."

"Very." He touched her breasts, using his palms to tease her nipples until they blossomed, firm and erect and excitingly hard. McCord lowered his head to kiss the rosy crests. "I'll never be able to get enough of you. If you really believe I could have let you walk away for good, you're out of your mind. Either that or you still don't know the extent of your power over me."

She laced her fingers through his hair, sighing softly as he slid her panty hose down her legs. "Do I have power over you, McCord?"

"An infinite amount." He straightened and smiled down at her. "Come here and I'll show you."

Pru stepped closer, her fingers on the buttons of his shirt, her mouth curved with feminine invitation. "No," she said, "I'll show you."

He grinned in wicked delight and anticipation as she deliberately began to take the initiative. It was only lately that she had become sure enough of her sensuality to do so, and it was still an infrequent occurrence, but McCord took great pleasure in having the tables turned occasionally. He got a kick out of having Pru turn into a sexy, assertive little bundle of demanding femininity.

Her fingers trailed tantalizingly over his bare chest as she undressed him. He could feel the faint trembling in her, and the knowledge that she was as aroused as he was nearly caused him to take back the lead. But he held himself in check, forcing himself to enjoy the unique pleasures to be found in the present situation.

There was a faint metallic clink as the buckle of his belt was undone and then the even softer rasp of his zipper. Pru's hand glided across the opening of the trousers and encountered the evidence of his arousal.

"Ah, McCord," she said with satisfaction, "you are a noble beast."

"You mean I'm in an advanced state of rut."

"Men are so literal."

"That's because we aren't built to be subtle." He caught her fingers when she would have moved her hand. He pressed her palm against himself, glorying in the intimate touch.

"You're right," Pru agreed. "Nothing subtle about you at all, is there?"

"You, I suppose, are much more discreet?"

"Naturally."

He laughed softly and slipped his fingers through the nest of curling hair between her thighs. When he found the spicy dampness, he drew his thumb through it and then over the tiny feminine bud.

Pru moaned and clutched at him, pressing her face into his shoulder.

"Tell me again about female subtlety. You couldn't hide your reaction from me if you tried, could you, sweetheart?" He stroked her softly.

"Probably not," she admitted. "You seem to have the magic touch where I'm concerned."

"I'm glad."

She smiled and took hold of his wrist to lead him across the carpet to the bed. There she pulled back the covers, slid between the sheets and reached up for him.

McCord groaned, going into her arms with a surge of desire that nearly overwhelmed him. She wrapped herself around him, pulling him close, welcoming him until he thought he would explode.

"You're so hot and sweet and sexy," he muttered against her breast as he drove himself into her and felt her legs curl around his hips. "So perfect for me. And you're all mine. What did I ever do without you?"

The question went unanswered as passion claimed them both. The world narrowed its focus to include only the depths of the bed, and McCord lost himself in the woman he had married.

It wasn't until a long while later when they both lay spent and damp with only a sheet pulled over their bodies that Pru reopened the subject of Laura Reynolds.

"Why didn't you fight harder, McCord? Your parents said you made one statement to the effect that Laura had lied and that the baby wasn't yours. You must have known they were in shock. Why didn't you yell until someone listened? You usually don't have that much trouble getting your point across."

He knew what she meant. He could have made a bigger scene three years ago. He could have shouted the truth until someone finally paid attention. "Pru, you have to understand. Laura really was pregnant."

"So?" She propped herself up on her elbow and looked down at him. "We know that much."

He studied her intent frown. She looked cute when she glared at him, he decided. "I knew I wasn't the father."

Pru nodded impatiently. "So?" she prodded again.

"That left open the question of who was."

Pru's eyes widened as the implications set in. "Oh, Lord. Didn't Laura ever tell you who had got her pregnant?"

McCord hesitated and then shrugged. "In the heat of her anger that night, she did give me a name."

"Whose?"

"My brother's," McCord said.

Pru sucked in her breath. "Kyle? She told you she'd been sleeping with Kyle?"

McCord nodded. "I had no reason to doubt her. She and Kyle had always been close, and I knew that Kyle found her attractive. But it had always been understood that Laura would probably marry me. She had no real interest in Kyle, I guess, because she knew I was the one who would inherit the reins of McCord Enterprises. Shortly before Laura died, Kyle and Carrie had begun dating. I knew my brother had fallen head over heels in love and was planning to marry."

"So you made one token protest and then shut up, is that it? You didn't want to ruin your brother's relationship with Carrie."

"I figured it would all work out eventually when the shock of Laura's death was behind us."

"But things didn't work out. You and your father quarreled. You got disinherited. A bad case of McCord stubbornness set in on both sides and voilà! Total disaster."

McCord looked up at her steadily. "If I hadn't got myself kicked out of the bosom of the family, I would never have met you. I, for one, do not consider the whole mess a total disaster."

"Oh." She blinked in surprise. Then she smiled. "Thank you, McCord."

"You're welcome. He waited expectantly to hear her say she loved him and was curiously irked when she went on to another topic of conversation.

"Do you think Kyle was the father of Laura's baby? Somehow that doesn't quite fit. I like Kyle. I can't see him having kept quiet about it for three years while the whole family turned against you."

"I don't know for certain who the father was," McCord said patiently. "Laura claimed it was Kyle, figuring I'd feel obliged to marry her to protect the family reputation. She also knew I would have done a hell of a lot for my brother."

"She really went the whole nine yards when she tried to manipulate you that night, didn't she? No wonder you came down on me like a landslide the day I tried to give you my puny little ultimatum."

"It wasn't exactly puny," McCord growled. "It was a major threat. I should have known that underneath that soft exterior, you've got nerves of steel."

"I was raised in Texas," Pru explained proudly.

"Uh-huh. By an aunt who doesn't make any allowances for weakness, I gather."

"Aunt Wilhelmina is a good person, but she does have a very forceful personality and an opinion on just about everything."

"I'm lucky she approves of me. Think she still will after she finds out I got you pregnant before I married you?" McCord grinned lazily, enjoying the flush on Pru's cheeks. In the shadows he couldn't quite see the fluctuating color, but with his fingertips he could definitely feel the warmth.

"Never mind my aunt," Pru said. "What about Kyle?"

"What about him?"

"Well, if we've decided he wasn't the father of Laura's baby, we've still got a problem."

McCord remembered the fury in Devin Blanchard's face as he'd tried to convince Pru that her husband had reneged on his responsibilities to Laura Reynolds. "No, we don't have a problem."

"But, McCord—"

"It all happened three years ago and the woman is dead, Pru. I agree with you. I don't think Kyle was the father. I said I had no reason to doubt Laura's statement that night, but that's not true. I should have doubted it on general principle. We'll probably never know who her lover was, and maybe it's for the best."

"I'm not so sure, McCord . . ."

He came up onto his elbow, pushing Pru back against the pillows. "I am sure," he said bluntly. "We're going to let the subject drop."

"Are we?" There was a hint of defiance in her voice.

McCord smiled faintly. "Yes," he repeated. "We are." He kissed her lips lingeringly, draining off some of her resentment. "Now go to sleep. You're a pregnant lady and you're supposed to take care of yourself."

"Hmm." A yawn spoiled the muted protest.

McCord lay back and gathered her against him. "There's just one more thing, Pru."

"What?" She was definitely sounding sleepy now.

"No more walks in the garden with Devin Blanchard. Not unless I'm along."

She stirred at his side, rubbing the sole of her foot down the inside of his leg. "Were you jealous?"

"Don't sound so pleased with yourself. Yes, I was jealous."

"Good." She was almost purring.

"Is that why you went out into the garden with him?" McCord asked curiously. "Because you wanted to make me jealous?"

Instantly she was contrite, just as he had known she would be. "No, of course not. We went looking for Hale and Evelyn. Devin thought he'd seen them wander out ahead of us. We decided we'd go out and chat with them while we all got some fresh air."

"Stay away from him, Pru." McCord heard the steel in his own voice and wondered if Pru heard it, too.

She yawned again and snuggled closer. "You *are* jealous."

"I'm a cautious man."

"Hah."

He tightened his hold on her. "Stop trying to provoke me. Go to sleep."

"All right. McCord?"

"Hmm?"

"Three years ago you knew for certain there was no way Laura's baby was yours. Did you ever wonder about the baby I'm carrying?"

"Not for a split second." The words were blunt and immediate, leaving absolutely no room for doubt. "You and the baby both belong to me."

"Yes, I know, but did you ever wonder?" she persisted.

"You are in a provoking mood tonight, aren't you?" He smiled in the darkness, vaguely aware of the smug certainty he had always felt around Pru. "It would be impossible for you to ever be unfaithful to me, and we both know it. It's not in you."

"I told Annie I trusted you completely," Pru murmured. "I'm glad we both trust each other so much."

"We know each other well enough to be sure of each other, I guess," McCord said matter-of-factly. It was only after the words were out of his mouth that he realized the implications of his statement. He'd never in his life fully trusted a woman the way he trusted Pru.

She was asleep in his arms within a few minutes. McCord cradled her protectively while he gazed thoughtfully at the ceiling. He decided that when he got back from Nebraska he would have a long talk with Devin Blanchard.

That decision made, he gazed at the ceiling a while longer and wondered when his wife would voluntarily confess her love. She did love him, McCord assured himself. She hadn't married him just because of the baby.

He knew it and she knew it. All he had to do was figure out a way to get her to admit it. More and more these days he wanted to hear the words.

SUNDAY EVENING Pru had the house to herself by six o'clock. Hale and Evelyn had left for home, and

McCord had reluctantly driven himself to the airport to leave for exotic Nebraska. The house, as usual, seemed quite empty without McCord in it. Pru spent the long summer evening in the garden. Then, mindful of her husband's injunction, she went to bed early.

The next day she went into the office and spent most of the time participating in the general mood of self-congratulation that permeated the atmosphere. J.P. was delighted with the success of the foundation's first big fund-raising event and couldn't stop talking about it.

"With the money that came rolling in Saturday night, we'll be able to add those second farm demonstration programs in a couple of those African countries," he informed everyone. "It will double our presence there. We'll reach twice as many people. Pru, I want you to know I had a phone call from your father-in-law this morning. I take back everything I said about him being tighter than the bark on a tree. He's writing out a real healthy check. Says anything his son is involved in is bound to be successful. Claims his boy always seems to land on his feet."

"I'm glad," Pru said, pleased by Hale's generosity. She knew the check represented much more than a charitable deduction for Hale McCord. It represented restored faith in his son.

"Couldn't have done it without you, Pru," J.P. said expansively. "You put the whole shootin' match together and made it work." Then he winked broadly. "By the way, McCord informed me he wants Bronson and Culpepper to start taking over more of the traveling."

"Really?"

"Yup. Says he's going to be a father and he wants to have plenty of time with his family." J.P. grinned. "I told him the news about being a father came kinda quick, seeing as how you two just got hitched a couple of weeks ago."

Pru coughed discreetly. "Yes, well, these things happen, J.P."

"Don't they just," he agreed blandly. "Good thing, too. Might have taken McCord a year or two to come around to the idea of marriage if he hadn't had a little pressure put on him. That man was happy as a pig in a mud waller in summer while he was living with you. Thought he had everything he needed, and I reckon he did. I knew it was going to take a jolt to make him wake up and do the right thing by you."

"It was a jolt, all right," Pru agreed dryly.

On the way home from work that afternoon, Pru decided to give in to the irresistible craving for pizza that had been consuming her for hours. She stopped by a take-out shop and ordered a pizza with everything to go. Then, with the aroma filling the car, she hurried home to gorge herself. This business of being pregnant could be fun once in a while. It had been years since she'd felt the urge to stuff herself with a pizza.

The thrill of illicit pizza faded rapidly when she spotted a strange car in the drive.

When she saw Devin Blanchard waiting on the front steps, Pru forgot about her dinner plans altogether. Vaguely she recalled McCord's soft warning the night of the ball. She had been almost asleep, but the steel in his words had made itself felt.

Stay away from Devin Blanchard.

11

"I CAME TO APOLOGIZE." Devin Blanchard trotted down the steps to take the fragrant box of pizza from Pru's arms.

Pru was still struggling with the idea of having him show up so unexpectedly. His apology jolted her further. "For what?"

His handsome mouth twisted ruefully. "For interfering in McCord family business the other night. I had no right to get involved as I'm sure some McCord will remind me when I show up at my office."

"You haven't been in to work since the ball?" Then she realized this was only Monday. Automatically Pru put her key into the front door lock.

"I called my secretary this morning and told her I was taking the day off. I wanted to do some thinking. And I wanted to talk to you."

Pru glanced at him quickly as she stepped into the hall. Short of grabbing her pizza out of his hands and slamming the door in his face, she didn't see any civilized way of keeping him out of the house. "What did you want to talk to me about?"

"First, as I said, to apologize." The door closed behind him, and he was alone with her in the house. Blanchard smiled. "I'm usually a lot more discreet than I was the other night, believe me."

"I believe you."

"Where do you want this?" He indicated the pizza.

"In the kitchen." She turned and led the way down the hall.

"As I was saying, I'm usually very careful when it comes to McCord family business. My only excuse is that I felt sorry for you."

"*Sorry* for me?"

He shrugged as he set the pizza carton down onto the tiled counter. "You're one of those women who brings out a man's protective instincts I guess." He paused. "Laura was like that."

"Thank you," Pru said tartly, "but I assure you I can take care of myself."

"That's what Laura thought, too."

"I'd rather not discuss her. Look, Devin, I think this has gone far enough. We really don't have much to say to each other. I accept your apology, but now I think you'd better leave."

He held up his hands as if to ward off her anger. "I'm sorry," he said again, shaking his head with a boyish smile. "I seem to keep putting my foot in my mouth. There was something else I wanted to tell you and then I'll leave."

"I don't want to hear it, Devin."

"This has got nothing to do with McCord family business, I swear. It's about something you said the other night at the ball."

"What was that?" she asked suspiciously. She didn't like being confined in the kitchen with him, she realized. Almost unconsciously she opened the back door and stepped out into the late afternoon warmth of the garden. Devin followed.

"You said that if I was unhappy working for the McCords, perhaps I should quit and start over somewhere else."

"I remember." She was a little more comfortable outside with him, Pru decided. Not quite so confined. But she still felt nervous. She began ambling along the vegetable plot. Devin fell into step beside her, his hands jammed into his pockets.

"At the time I told you I didn't want to walk away from such a sweet setup. I'm making good money, lots of perks and—"

"And you're near the seat of power," she finished for him. "You said you liked that."

"I thought it was the next best thing to being the man in charge."

"But not quite the same thing as being the man in charge."

"No," he agreed. "Not quite. I thought a lot about what you said after I got home yesterday, however. It made sense. I don't know why I hadn't figured it out for myself. I've decided you were right. I really shouldn't be working for a McCord. Any McCord. Especially not after what happened three years ago."

"Why were you so upset about what happened three years ago, Devin?" Pru asked quietly. "I mean, I know it was a terrible tragedy, but why did you take it so personally?"

He hesitated. "Probably because I admired Case so much. Maybe I'd put him on a pedestal. I couldn't believe he would treat Laura the way he did. She was such a beautiful, loving woman."

"He didn't do anything to Laura," Pru snapped. "She had been cheating on him, and he didn't intend to be manipulated. When he told her that, she lost her temper and climbed into a car. What happened next was strictly her own fault."

"Do you really believe that?" He gave her a pitying look.

"Yes, I really believe it!"

"All right, all right. Calm down. It all happened a long time ago, and maybe it's time to put it behind us. In any event, I didn't come here to argue, I promise. I just wanted you to know that I think you were right. I shouldn't be working for McCord Enterprises. I'm going to hand in my notice tomorrow morning. I thought you'd like to know how much influence you've had on me. You seem to have had a lot of influence on the McCords, too. I never thought the family would ever accept Case back into the fold."

Something clicked in Pru's mind. "You mean you hoped they never would accept him back," she said with quiet insight. "You wanted them to punish one another indefinitely, didn't you?"

The boyish expression vanished from Devin's eyes as if it had never existed. It was replaced by a vicious bitterness that made Pru gasp.

"They deserved to be punished," Devin snarled. "They were all responsible for what happened. There was no way to hurt the McCords financially, but I knew the family rift was eating all of them alive. That was some satisfaction."

Pru drew a deep breath and came to a halt near a tree. Steve had left a rake propped against the trunk, she noticed. McCord would be irritated, as usual. She stood looking out toward the ocean, her fingers trembling slightly as she put together the rest of the facts. "It was your baby Laura was carrying, wasn't it, Devin?"

"Yes, it was mine," Blanchard bit out through clenched teeth. "Laura gave herself to me. *Me*, not Case McCord. She never allowed Case to touch her. She used to laugh about that, you know. We both did. McCord thought he was going to be marrying a picture-perfect angel. It gave me great pleasure to know that every time I took Laura to bed I was screwing Case McCord's fiancée."

"You used her. You didn't love her. For you she was just a means of getting even with the McCords."

"Don't waste any of your sympathy on Laura. She knew exactly what she was doing. She got a kick out of sleeping with me behind her fiancée's back. It was a real thrill for her. Laura didn't like being bored, and waiting around to marry into the McCord clan had grown extremely boring for her. What's more, she was beginning to fear that she was going to be bored after she married, too. The McCords are wealthy and powerful, but they live a quiet life. They're not socialites or jet-setters. After all, they're only one generation away from picking beans, as Laura used to say. She decided to have a little fun on the side. If you want to know the truth, I think she fully intended to continue the affair with me after she got married."

"But she would never have married you, right? And that's what you really wanted. Because she was going to inherit a major portion of McCord Enterprises. Marrying Laura would have given you the position in McCord Enterprises you always wanted to have."

Devin's eyes hardened. The breeze off the sea ruffled his hair slightly as he stood staring down at Pru's profile. "Yes, I wanted to marry her. They accepted her as a daughter, and ultimately she stood to inherit her father's share of the company. If I was Laura's husband, I would have gained a sizable chunk of control in McCord Enterprises. But Laura wasn't interested. She didn't want half the pie when by marrying a McCord she could have all of it. The little bitch. She used me as much as I tried to use her. But she wasn't about to give up her chance of being a McCord. She knew what she wanted. What's more, she always got it."

"Until the night McCord told her he was breaking off the engagement."

"She must have been out of her head with rage that night," Devin said softly. "Laura had a violent temper, although she was careful to conceal it most of the time. Didn't fit the angel image she always presented to the McCords. When she first learned she was pregnant, she planned to have an abortion. Then she decided that she might be able to use the baby to prod Case into marrying her. I think she knew he was slipping through her greedy little fingers. There had been plenty of signs. She panicked. She had tried to get him to make love to her so that she could claim the baby was his, but I guess he was already suspicious. Or maybe he was just tired of her little sex games. She'd kept him dangling so long he probably just lost interest. Laura thought she had all the McCords on the end of her puppet strings. She used to laugh about how easy it was to get them to do what she wanted. But things went wrong when she started pushing Case."

"So she lost her temper and tried a rash, stupid tactic. She burst into tears and threw herself into Mc-Cord's arms, claiming Kyle had seduced her. She thought McCord would feel obliged to make up for his brother's actions." Pru shook her head in silent disgust.

"It was a reasonable assumption. She knew Case would do a lot for Kyle. She'd always been very good at manipulating the McCords and she assumed she could predict their responses."

"But her luck ran out the night she tried to nail McCord with another man's baby. After that, she knew she was in trouble. She'd burned her bridges."

"She phoned me after McCord left her apartment that night. Said she had to see me. Claimed I had to help her."

Pru closed her eyes. "Then she climbed into a car and headed for your home at nearly a hundred miles an hour. What a sad story."

Devin's face was grim with remembered satisfaction. "She managed to extract some revenge against the McCords at the end, though. I was at the hospital that night. I heard her, and I saw the looks on the faces of Hale and Evelyn when she told them McCord had seduced and abandoned her, leaving her pregnant and desperate."

"Yes, she certainly got her revenge, didn't she? Three years' worth." Pru felt a rush of pity for all concerned.

"It's not enough, Pru. Not nearly enough."

She froze at the dangerous bitterness underlying the words. Her fingers dug into the bark of the tree, and she turned her head to stare at Devin. "What are you talking about? It's over. Let it go, Devin."

"Not yet. Not until I've proven to Case McCord that you're no better than Laura was. He thinks he's so damn smart to have finally found a woman who believes in him completely, no questions asked. A woman who gives him all her silly, blind loyalty. He thinks you're at opposite ends of the spectrum from Laura. But he's wrong."

"Get out of here, Devin." Frightened now, Pru tried to put every ounce of command she possessed into her voice.

"Case always lands on his feet. When he lost his whole inheritance, he seemed to take it in stride. He just walked away and didn't look back. It didn't even matter to him."

"You're wrong, Devin. Losing contact with his family mattered to him."

Blanchard waved that aside. "The real loss was the power and prestige he had as the heir to McCord Enterprises. You'd have thought the corporation was so much confetti, the way he reacted when his father kicked him out. McCord created a new career for himself, found a new woman and now he doesn't even want any part of McCord Enterprises. He's always been lucky. Always got what he wanted. He even escaped having to marry Laura after she made a fool of him behind his back. But I'm going to make sure he knows he wasn't so fortunate when he married you. Case McCord is going to learn his luck isn't infallible. You had fun making your grand announcement the other night at the fountain, didn't you? Well, let's see how long McCord goes on believing the baby is his after he knows some other man has had you."

Pru jumped back instinctively when Devin reached for her. Unfortunately she came up against the tree trunk and couldn't move aside quickly enough to avoid Devin's grasping hands. His fingers closed around her shoulders. When she looked up into his face, she saw nothing but hard, bitter anger. Years of it.

"Let me go, Devin," she snapped. "This isn't going to give you the revenge you want."

"I'm willing to give it a try. You must be pretty damn good in bed for McCord to marry you after he'd been living with you for three months. Laura would be furious if she knew you'd manipulated him into marrying you by using the baby. She thought she was a brilliant manipulator."

"There is one major difference between Laura's situation and mine," Pru gasped, struggling to free herself. "The baby I'm carrying is McCord's, and he knows it."

"How can he be sure?"

Pru was shocked. "He trusts me. He knows I would never cheat on him."

"He won't be so sure of that after today, will he? I'll make certain he knows I've had you, Pru. I'll give him a blow-by-blow account."

"He'll kill you."

"He won't be able to touch me. Besides, it's far more likely he'll take out his anger on you. You're the one who betrayed him. *Just as Laura did.* He'll never forgive you for making a fool of him, Pru."

He was forcing her to the ground beneath the tree. Pru opened her mouth to scream, and instantly Devin clamped a hand over her lips. She twisted furiously in his grasp, using her nails to claw at him.

"Stop it, you little bitch. It won't do any good. You'll only hurt yourself."

He sprawled on top of her, pinning her struggling body with his heavy legs. He kept one hand across her mouth as his other hand went to the front of her dress.

Pru panicked. She was rapidly slipping beyond coherent thought. She only knew she had to get free regardless of the cost. Dimly she remembered the rake that had been propped against the tree trunk. Her hand groped for it as she prayed she wasn't too far away to reach it.

Her fingers encountered the metal prongs just as Devin began tugging at the material of her dress. The fabric was tougher than Pru would have expected. Her assailant was having to work at the task of trying to tear it.

Pru clutched at the rake, seeking a useful grip. She managed to bring the long wooden handle sharply down on Devin's back. It didn't do much damage, but it startled him.

"What the hell . . . ? Damn you!"

His hand came free of her mouth as he reached around to wrest the rake from her fingers. Pru screamed.

"Shut up!"

He tried to cover her mouth again, and as soon as he released the grip on her hand, she grabbed the metal prongs of the rake. This time, she vowed silently, she would do more damage.

Devin yelled and jerked away from his victim as he suddenly became aware of what Pru intended to do. The steel prongs were only an inch away from his back as he rolled free and jumped to his feet.

Pru scrambled to her feet, clutching the rake. She held the implement out in front of her as she backed quickly toward the safety of the house. If she could get inside and slam the door, she would be all right. She could call the police. Devin was coming toward her, his eyes burning with fury. He was waiting for an opening, and Pru knew it. One false step and her makeshift weapon would be wrenched from her hands.

"Stay away from me," she warned.

She had almost reached the kitchen door when it swung open behind her. Pru jumped, swinging around in relief to greet whoever it was who had unwittingly come to her rescue. Expecting Steve or Martha, it came as a shock to see McCord filling the doorway.

"McCord!" she breathed in overwhelming relief. Throwing down the rake, she raced for the safety of his arms.

He caught her as she flew to him, but he didn't hold her. "Get inside." He was shoving her behind him into the kitchen before she could speak. Then he turned to confront Devin Blanchard.

"McCord, no," Pru said urgently as she realized his intention. "I'll call the police."

"Go ahead and call them," he said easily as he started forward. "I've got time to finish this before they get here."

Pru's fingers tightened around the doorknob. She wanted to stop what was going to happen next, but she knew there was nothing she could do. She could only hope McCord wouldn't get hurt.

She should have known better.

McCord always landed on his feet.

IT WAS A LONG TIME before Pru got to her pizza. The police had come and gone, taking a sullen Devin Blanchard with them. Pru and McCord had both made statements and assured the officers they would press charges. All told, some two hours passed before Pru pulled her pizza back out of the refrigerator where she had stored it while McCord dealt with the police. She was starving, she realized.

She turned on the oven and shoved the pizza inside just as McCord stalked into the kitchen. He looked none the worse for wear after the short, violent confrontation with Devin Blanchard. The same couldn't be said about Blanchard. But Pru didn't particularly care about Blanchard's condition. The cops hadn't seemed unduly alarmed, either.

"Do you want some pizza?" Pru asked cheerfully as McCord halted behind her.

"What I want," McCord said grimly, "is an explanation of why you let Blanchard into the house. I told you to stay away from him, Pru."

"Is this going to be an inquisition?"

"Yes."

She smiled, folded her arms and leaned back against the counter to face him. "Then we can start with the question of what you're doing home a day early."

He glowered at her, running his fingers through his hair in annoyance. "I got through with the Nebraska assignment sooner than I expected. There's no great mystery involved. I came rushing back to hearth and home only to discover my wife fighting off an attacker who should never have been allowed into the house in the first place. Hell, Pru, have you any idea of what I felt when I opened the kitchen door and saw what was happening?"

"I know," she said, her voice gentling as she saw the raw emotion in his eyes. "I'm sorry."

He was not in a mood to be placated. "You should be. Are you sure you're all right?"

"I'm sure. I feel fine. He didn't have a chance to hurt me, McCord."

His mouth crooked faintly. "You looked like you were doing a fairly good job of defending yourself."

"Thank you," she murmured. "I come from Spot, Texas, remember. You learn things in Spot, Texas."

"Why was he here, Pru?"

She sighed. "He said he came to apologize for that scene at the fountain the other night. He claimed I'd made him realize he really shouldn't be working for McCord Enterprises. Said I'd made him see the light."

"And you bought that, hook, line and sinker?"

"Well, I certainly didn't expect him to attack me," she flared. "I thought he just wanted to talk."

"I told you to stay away from him."

"But you didn't tell me why, McCord. You didn't tell me that Blanchard was the father of Laura's baby."

He sucked in his breath. "He admitted it?"

"Oh, yes. He admitted it." Pru frowned. "Didn't you know?"

McCord stopped his restless pacing and sprawled into a chair at the kitchen table. "The other night after the ball I began to wonder if he might have been Laura's lover. He was too intent on warning you away from me. I saw his face that night at the fountain. He was too—" McCord lifted one shoulder, searching for the words "—emotionally involved, I guess you could say."

"He was that, all right. He hated you and your family."

McCord stared at her. "I intended to have it out with him when I got back from this trip." He shook his head. "Damn it, Pru, he worked for us for years. We trusted him completely."

"It wasn't enough. He always felt like an outsider. He didn't just want to be a friend of the family, he wanted to be a member of the family, and there was no way that could happen. He resented everything you had, and at the same time he couldn't bring himself to walk away from the cushy position he had. He thought for a while that marrying Laura was the answer. The McCords treated her like a daughter, and she was due to inherit a chunk of McCord Enterprises. But Laura wasn't about to marry an outsider. She was intent on being a McCord."

"She wasn't in love with me," McCord said thoughtfully.

"I'm afraid love had nothing to do with it."

"She played her charming little ingenue games for me and my family while she amused herself with Blanchard on the side." McCord grimaced. "I'd known from the beginning that she wasn't exactly in love with me. But I thought we had a lot in common, and I assumed a marriage between us would work. I cared for her, just as everyone else in the family did. It wasn't until after the engagement when I started seriously thinking about what it would mean to live with her that I began wondering if it was wise for us to marry. She didn't want to talk about any doubts on the subject, though. Probably because she herself wasn't having any. After all, she'd already made up her mind about what she wanted."

"She wanted to secure her place in the family."

"She should have been more careful," McCord pointed out.

"About getting pregnant? I gather that was an accident. One she intended to remedy until she decided she might be able to use it to prod you into marriage. Apparently she had begun to worry about losing you. Unfortunately for her, you weren't easy to prod. You don't take kindly to being manipulated."

McCord swore softly under his breath. "Let's not get started on that subject."

"Suits me." Pru smiled as she bent down to open the oven and remove her pizza. She sniffed appreciatively. "Almost as good as new."

McCord eyed the pizza dubiously. "What have you got on there?"

"Jalapeño peppers, anchovies, olives, onions and hot sauce. I call it a J. P. Arlington Foundation Special.

Want some?" She carried it over to the table and set it down.

"You're trying to distract me. In fact, I think you already have distracted me. I'm supposed to be lecturing you on the foolishness of disobeying my clear-cut instructions."

"Darn right. You think I want to sit here eating this fabulous pizza while listening to you rant and rave about how I shouldn't have let Devin Blanchard through the front door?" She sat down and shoveled two fat slices onto the plates she had set out earlier. "You shouldn't yell at a pregnant lady, anyway. Speaking of yelling . . ."

"What about it?"

"I want you to promise not to yell at Steve about leaving the garden tools lying around for at least a month."

"I never yell," he reminded her.

"Well, I don't want you lecturing him about the matter, then. In fact, I want you to remember to thank him for leaving that rake propped against the tree."

McCord groaned. "I guess I do owe him something for that piece of carelessness, don't I?"

"Yes, you do." She handed him his pizza.

McCord's mouth twitched as he accepted his plate. He glanced down at the pizza and then back at his wife's face. She looked at him, her eyes sparkling as she closed her small teeth around a huge bite of pizza and began to chew. "You never gave me my standard welcome-home kiss," McCord complained suddenly.

Pru stopped chewing, her mouth still full. "Is that right?" Her voice was muffled. "I seem to remember flying to you on winged feet not more than two hours ago."

"Throwing yourself into my arms as you flee an attacker doesn't count."

"Oh." She swallowed the bite of pizza, got up and came around the table to sit in his lap. "I hope you like jalapeños, anchovies, olives and onions." She kissed him soundly.

His arm came around her waist. "I love jalapeños, anchovies, olives and onions. And I love you."

She went very still for a moment, her eyes shining. "Do you, McCord?"

"I've loved you from the beginning," he said quietly. "I don't know why it took me so damn long to say the words."

"You'd been severely traumatized by your experience with Laura," Pru explained generously. "You weren't about to let yourself get manipulated by a woman. I think in your subconscious mind you equated love with the kind of weakness that might leave you open to being manipulated."

"Is that right?" He looked at her admiringly. "Did you figure that out all on your own, or did you take a correspondence course in psychology?"

"I figured it out all on my own."

"You must have spent a lot of time analyzing me."

"Oh, I did," she assured him. "Endless hours."

"Why?"

She smiled and hugged him. "Because I love you, naturally."

He held her close, his mouth in her hair. "I was wondering when you were going to admit it freely."

"You must have known since the beginning."

"I did, or at least I hoped I did. But it's always nice to hear the words."

She shook her head ruefully. "You were always so sure of me."

"You're not very good at hiding your emotions, sweetheart. Every time you look at me I can feel you loving me. I've never known anything like it in my life. Whenever I was away on a trip, all I could think about was getting home so I could have you back in my arms. I'd sit there on the plane coming home from wherever I'd just been and I'd think about how soon I'd be able to tell you all about the trip and what I'd seen and what plans I'd made for foundation activities in that particular region. And then I'd think about sharing a drink with you and a good meal while I unwound and listened to you tell me about what had been happening back here while I was gone. Finally we'd go to bed together, and after we made love you'd curl up beside me and we'd go to sleep. Very simple, very comfortable."

"It all sounds very married."

"But it wasn't. Not quite. And that's where I went wrong, Pru. I should have married you the first day I saw you."

"Yes," Pru agreed, "you should have. It's just like Aunt Wilhelmina always said, 'Give a man free whiskey long enough and he'll get used to the notion of not having to pay for it. It's tough to collect after he's drunk his fill.'"

McCord groaned. "Are you going to throw your aunt's words in my face for the rest of our lives?"

Pru shook her head, grinning. "No, because as it happens I'm glad we did things the way we did."

"Glad!" He gave her an astounded look.

"Uh-huh. This way I got to experience the thrill of an illicit affair. I shall have such wonderfully racy tales to tell my grandchildren."

"Living with a man these days hardly qualifies as an illicit affair," McCord pointed out. "More like a normal event for two people who are as attracted to each other as we are."

"You can say that because you're from California. Those of us who come from Spot, Texas, view these things differently. Three months of being your live-in lover was just about the most exciting thing that's ever happened to me, McCord."

"I can only hope you're not going to be bored now that the illicit thrill is gone." His eyes were gleaming.

"The wonderful thing about being married to you, McCord, is that it's even better than being your live-in lover."

"I'm glad you feel that way, because there's no going back to the old days." There was fascinating determination in McCord's dark eyes. "You're my wife now. I'll never let you go."

Pru smiled, all her love shining in her gaze. "That's just what I wanted to hear." She got up off his lap and went around to sit down on her side of the table. "Have some more pizza before it gets cold."

He grinned. "Does it strike you that we're both being rather casual about declaring our love to each other?"

"I expect it's because we've been living together long enough to know we both mean what we're saying," Pru said complacently.

"No excitement?"

She shook her head. "No fears or uncertainties," she corrected gently.

"You're right." McCord smiled. "It's nice to be sure of each other. Besides, the exciting part comes later. In bed."

Much later that evening when Pru came out of the bathroom in her nightgown she found McCord lying naked, propped against the pillows with his arms folded behind his head.

He watched her come through the doorway with his usual gleaming, quietly possessive expression. Pru smiled, thinking that some things never change. He had got in the habit of looking at her like this after the first time they had made love. She had a feeling he would still have that look in his eyes the night they celebrated their fiftieth wedding anniversary. It was a pleasant thought.

Pru stopped at the foot of the bed, gazing down at him. The sheet was at his waist, revealing the strong lines of his chest and hinting at the hardness of his lower body.

"What are you thinking, Pru?"

"I'm thinking about what a sexy man I married."

He grinned, thoroughly pleased. His eyes flicked briefly to where the sheet barely covered his arousal. "You've always had this effect on me."

"I'm glad," she said happily. She came around to her side of the bed and climbed in beside him. "It's only fair, considering what you do to me with just a glance or a touch. I love you so much, McCord."

The laughter went out of his eyes to be replaced by the familiar hunger. He reached for her, drawing her into his arms and tangling his legs with hers until they were wound together in a deeply sensual embrace.

"My sweet, beautiful, Pru." He kissed her throat, letting his hand slide over her breast to her hip.

"You make me feel beautiful, McCord," she whispered as she touched her lips to his chest. "When you hold me I feel exotic and gorgeous and sexy."

He laughed huskily. "That's because you are all of those things. You turn to liquid fire in my arms. But it's nothing compared to the way you make me feel."

"How's that?"

"As if I'll explode."

"I'm glad." Boldly she trailed her fingertips down to his thigh and then cupped him intimately. In her palm he was heavy and hard as steel. But the steel was sheathed in velvet, and she was already aching to know the feel of him inside her. She felt his fingers twisting gently in the softness at the juncture of her thighs, and she shivered.

McCord muttered something hot and dark and sensual against her breast and probed her with an excruciatingly slow, teasing movement of his hand. When she cried out and clung to him, he gasped and moved on top of her. The weight of him was deliciously exciting. Pru's senses whirled with the glittering sensations that were pouring through her.

"How could you have believed for even one moment that I wouldn't come after you if you left me?" Mc-

Cord's voice was raw with emotion as he lifted his head to stare down into her eyes. "I would have followed you to the ends of the world. You belong to me, Pru. Swear you'll never leave me again."

"Never," she vowed. Her arms laced around his neck, holding him close. "In my heart, I never did leave you."

His smile was wicked with latent male satisfaction. "That's what I told myself that day I found you beside your sister's pool. I took one look at the hope and relief I saw in your eyes and I knew you were still mine, that you'd always be mine. All I had to do was make sure you knew that. I figured putting a ring on your finger was as good a way to do that as any."

"Does that mean you are now taking credit for having manipulated me into marriage, not vice versa?"

"Like J.P. says, once you had my attention, there was no stopping me from seeing the light of sweet logic and reason." He covered her mouth with his own and surged into her, filling her with his hard, throbbing steel sheathed in velvet.

Pru sucked in her breath under the sensual impact and then she wrapped her husband in her arms and gave herself up to the wonders of married life.

SEVERAL MONTHS LATER Pru lay back against the pillows of her hospital room bed and handed tiny James Hale McCord to his father. McCord took his sleeping son from his wife and laid the baby carefully in the cradle near the bed. For a long moment he stood gazing down at the infant, examining once more the miniature perfection of the little fingers and toes.

"He's something else, isn't he?" McCord said, not for the first time. He had been saying similar words ever since he'd held his wife's hand in the delivery room and agonized with her as James Hale had made his appearance in the world.

"He's going to look just like you."

"Yeah." McCord was clearly pleased by the idea. He stood looking down at his son for a moment longer and then he came across to the bed. "I love you, Mrs. McCord."

Pru smiled and touched his cheek. "I love you, too."

"I'm going to take very good care of you and our son."

"I never doubted it for a moment," she assured him softly.

McCord's fingers laced through hers, and he kissed the palm of her hand. At that moment the door swung open so abruptly that Pru jumped. McCord glanced up in mild annoyance as he saw who stood in the doorway.

"Do you always have to make an entrance, J.P.?"

J.P., resplendent in lemon yellow from head to toe, grinned broadly. "Only when I have a surprise. Look who I've got with me, Pru." He stood aside, bowing with a grand flourish as a magnificently built woman in her mid-fifties swept into the room. Tall, handsome, with flashing blue eyes and a severely neat bun of graying chestnut hair, the lady was as much a sight to behold as J.P.

Pru stared in amazement and then she laughed. "Aunt Wilhelmina! What are you doing here?"

"Why, I've come to see the baby, of course. This charming Texas gentleman was kind enough to invite me. And thank the good Lord he did. At the rate things were going, the hog wallers would have frozen over before I got an invitation from you, girl." Wilhelmina's handsome eyes were much softer than her accusation.

"Not fair, Aunt Willy. I told you the last time I called you that we'd want you to come see the baby as soon as possible."

J.P. chuckled. "When you work for J. P. Arlington, the possible happens real quick. It's just the impossible that takes a while. How do you like my little surprise, Pru?"

"I'm surprised," she agreed with a grin. "Aunt Willy, this is McCord."

"Hello, Aunt Willy," McCord said easily. His eyes were alight with humor.

Wilhelmina examined McCord with slow deliberation. "I knew it," she finally announced. "Slicker than a greased hog on ice. Congratulations, Pru. You did all right for yourself. You're a lucky gal, and I hope you know it."

"Yes, Aunt Willy. I'm aware of it."

"Good. Now let's see this baby." She advanced across the room to stand beside the crib. "Hmm. Big, isn't he? Not much chance of passing this little guy off as a couple of months premature."

Pru swallowed her amusement. "We weren't even going to try, Aunt Willy."

"Just as well. One small lie always leads to another, and first thing you know you're in more trouble than a dog who's cornered a skunk. Besides," Wilhelmina declared, "it doesn't much matter if you anticipated things a bit, Pru. Your man did right by you in the end, and that's all that counts."

"I'm glad you approve, Aunt Willy. Are you going up to Pasadena to see Annie and Tony while you're on the coast?"

"Of course," Wilhelmina said, "but there's no rush."

Pru coughed a little, wondering how McCord was going to tolerate having Wilhelmina in the house for a few days. "Uh, we're going to be quite busy for a while, Aunt Willy. I'm afraid McCord and I won't have a lot of spare time to show you around La Jolla and San Diego."

"No need to worry about that," J.P. announced. "I hereby claim the privilege of showing Miss Wilhelmina the magnificent California coast. Thought we'd look around San Diego for a few days and then take a leisurely drive up toward Pasadena. Wilhelmina tells me she's never seen Disneyland."

Pru's eyes widened in amazement. "Is that right, Aunt Willy?"

"I told you he was a most charming Texas gentleman." Wilhelmina gave J.P. a fond glance. It was returned in kind. "I can't wait to start the sight-seeing."

"We've got reservations for dinner in an hour," J.P. said happily. "We'd probably best be on our way. Mustn't tire the new mother."

"Right you are." Wilhelmina went over to the bed and dropped one of her brusquely affectionate kisses of greeting on Pru's forehead. "Fine young son you have, Pru. And a fine husband. You take care of both of them now, you hear?"

"I hear."

"Good. See you in the morning, dear. Get plenty of rest." Wilhelmina patted Pru's hand and started toward the door.

"Aunt Willy?" Pru wasn't sure what to say next. She needn't have worried. Wilhelmina paused in the doorway as J.P. took her arm.

"Don't you worry about a thing, dear," Wilhelmina said airily. "There aren't a great number of advantages to being my age, but there are one or two. Chief among them is that I'm not likely to get pregnant by accident."

She swept through the door and disappeared down the hall on J.P.'s arm before Pru could think of a response. As the door closed behind her aunt, Pru shut her mouth and turned to meet her husband's laughing eyes.

"I think J.P. has met his match," McCord said. "It's only fair. After all, I've met mine."

He leaned down and kissed his wife with a love and a passion that proved his point beyond a shadow of a doubt.

Barbara Delinsky strikes again!

Remember Victoria Lesser, the offbeat, warmhearted widow who couldn't help meddling in her friends lives—and love affairs?

She sent Neil and Deirdre to the same "deserted island" when they needed to get away from it all (*The Real Thing*, #130).

She tricked Leah into moving up north, to a cabin that had burned down three months before! Naturally Leah *had* to take shelter with Garrick.... (*Twelve Across*, #144).

Now the tide has turned, as Victoria's grateful, happily-ever-after friends send *her* off on a romantic adventure she'll never forget. Sailing into the sunset, looking for buried treasure—surely that'll give Victoria enough to do without meddling in yet another couple's romance . . . or will it?

Don't miss

⤙ *A Single Rose* ⤚

Temptation #150, coming next month from Barbara Delinsky. . . and Harlequin!

Harlequin Temptation

COMING NEXT MONTH

ATTRACTIVE, SPACE SAVING BOOK RACK

Display your most prized novels on this handsome and sturdy book rack. The hand-rubbed walnut finish will blend into your library decor with quiet elegance, providing a practical organizer for your favorite hard-or soft-covered books.

Only $9.95

Approximately 16" x 8" when assembled

Assembles in seconds!

To order, rush your name, address and zip code, along with a check or money order for $10.70* ($9.95 plus 75¢ postage and handling) payable to *Harlequin Reader Service*:

> Harlequin Reader Service
> Book Rack Offer
> 901 Fuhrmann Blvd.
> P.O. Box 1325
> Buffalo, NY 14269-1325
>
> *Offer not available in Canada.*

*New York residents add appropriate sales tax.

BKR-1R

New This spring

Harlequin Category Romance Specials!

New Mix

4 Regencies—for more wit, tradition, etiquette... and romance

2 Gothics—for more suspense, drama, adventure... and romance

Regencies

A Hint of Scandal by Alberta Sinclair
She was forced to accept his offer of marriage, but could she live with her decision?

The Primrose Path by Jean Reece
She was determined to ruin his reputation and came close to destroying her own!

Dame Fortune's Fancy by Phyllis Taylor Pianka
She knew her dream of love could not survive the barrier of his family tradition....

The Winter Picnic by Dixie McKeone
All the signs indicated they were a mismatched couple, yet she could not ignore her heart's request....

Gothics

Mirage on the Amazon by Mary Kistler
Her sense of foreboding did not prepare her for what lay in waiting at journey's end....

Island of Mystery by Margaret M. Scariano
It was the perfect summer job, or so she thought—until it became a nightmare of danger and intrigue.

Don't miss any of them!

PATRICIA MATTHEWS

America's First Lady of Romance upholds her long standing reputation as a bestselling romance novelist with...

Caught in the steamy heat of America's New South, Rebecca Trenton finds herself torn between two brothers—she yearns for one but a dark secret binds her to the other.

 **WORLDWIDE LIBRARY**

Take 4 best-selling love stories FREE
Plus get a FREE surprise gift!